The Japanese Cook

The Japanese Cook

A Novel

Brooke Biaz

Parlor Press
Anderson, South Carolina
www.parlorpress.com

Parlor Press LLC, Anderson, South Carolina, USA

S A N: 2 5 4 - 8 8 7 9

Library of Congress Cataloging-in-Publication Data on File

978-1-60235-582-8 (paperback)
978-1-60235-583-5 (PDF)
978-1-60235-597-5 (ePub
978-1-60235-579-8 (Kindle)

Cover image: "Spring Kitchen Line-Up." Photo by Brooke Lark on
    Unsplash. https://unsplash.com/photos/08bOYnH_r_E
Cover design by David Blakesley.
Printed on acid-free paper.

1 2 3 4 5
First Edition

Parlor Press, LLC is an independent publisher of scholarly and trade
titles in print and multimedia formats. This book is available in
paper and digital formats from Parlor Press on the World Wide Web
at http://www.parlorpress.com or through online and brick-and-
mortar bookstores. For submission information or to find out about
Parlor Press publications, write to Parlor Press, 3015 Brackenberry
Drive, Anderson, SC 29621, or e-mail editor@parlorpress.com.

Contents

A truly great cook is a witch who finds, no matter how hard she tries to resist, she can only conjure up joy.

—*Meika Fuji*

There is an old Japanese saying that says, *Kono kudamono o okurimono yō ni tsutsunde itadakemasu ka* ("A scar tells the history not of an injury but of a moment of survival").

The Japanese Cook

KOJI

Suzuki-no-arai

Nobuko told me that in Japan there were kitchens that sing like birds. That whistle and chirp. Kitchens all bright and lively like the bedrooms of infants or the gardens of godmothers. Kitchens full of pride and polish where cupboards shine and pots clank. Kitchens for visits and talking. Bubbling and steaming and stringing out aromas from latchless door to latticed window. Lace curtained kitchens. *Iro wa chairo desu.* Clear water kitchens. Kitchens of honey and wholemeal. Homey, unpolluted kitchens. Kitchens built in avenues of vines and forests of plum colored palms. Kitchens with music. The joyful humming ovens. The steady burbling soups. The metronome counting of egg time. Hatching kitchens. There are kitchens we know that are the favorites in the house. That dismiss lounge rooms outright. That make dining rooms irrelevant. That act as foyers and vestibules. That are invested with vestibuleness, in fact. Like toothy smiles or welcome mats. Like the pleasant shake-down of a sheltered doorway in a tropical rainstorm or the deep lie of a downy duvet on a crisp cold sheet. These kinds of kitchens. The well-rounded and fun. The kitchens that recur in memory. The one where your scraped knee was carefully bathed. The photograph of you on a kitchen stool, dressed as a dog for some Nursery School Fancy Dress. Or where your father lifted your mother onto his shoulders when she said she had grown fat and he insisted she hadn't. And there they were teetering back and forth in that kitchen between the neat pine chopping block and the glistening silver draining board. You as small as a mouse below, watching their lined faces like the territories of a map shifting before you, one nation merging immeasurably with another, the mountains of terror flowing into the ravines of happiness. Your parents made human. We know these kitchens well. The kitchen with no boundaries. The running through kitchen, your mother calling to you to slow down, but laughing all the while. Your father washing his car-greased hands in your mother's suds. Those growls of loving disproval. *Omakase shimasu.* Your safe site beneath the breakfast table, small and meek beneath a year's amassed junk mail, the torn envelopes of paid bills, the crepe fliers for festivals and *o-matsuri*, your report cards, your mother's dental appointments. There are those kitchens that live life themselves. That give over to it their fast-moving consumption. That are proud and pleasant and rounded. Great lived kitchens that are wooden and steel. Kitchens with color and contemporaneousness. The *gassho*-style farmhouse kitchen, floral and firm. The condo kitchen with its white melamine and merciless doors. The kitchen of your Japanese teacher, textured with too-gold frames of her departed husband. Clean, pine scented kitchens. Tabby cat kitchens. Rambling kitchens. Heat in the hearth. A pin-cushion of bricks rising to the copper flue. Notes there: "See Akiro at 1.30." "Osamu called. Wants to talk." Scattered kitchen messages: "Take duck out of the freezer", "Clean bar-

becue." Kitchens with purpose and agility. The manly kitch-
en, half-empty with anticipation. The bachelorette pad, kitch-
en trimmed like a porpoise in a petticoat, grey tiles glinting
with water, pure white plastic bag in the swing-top bin, grin
of toothy joy from a rack of improbably useful spices. There
are those kitchens we know that reflect, perhaps even make,
their cooks, their *rakugo*. Good cooks. Great cooks even. Who
are not limited to any national cuisine. Who use their Japanese kitchens as tools. Who fill the atmosphere with speculation. Who are inventive and genuine. Who love the site of a
meal in construction. Who spend their waking hours in the
company of haute cuisine. Who want you to enjoy. Who want
you to love. Who admire your tastebuds as if wanting to pat
an old well-loved dog. Who care for your children. Who will
cook for them especially, if need be. Who will fillet a joint or
trim a cut. Just for you. Because you will it. Who coax and
encourage and bow down to the quirks of food. Who make
it their life. Give it life. Cook and cater and cull their living
into the realm of cuisine where nothing is permanent or perfect, no one completely satisfied, no meal ever quite over. But
where everything is possible. There are those cooks we know.
The good and the great *rakugo*. Who fill kitchens with fancy
and fineness. Who are the purveyors of substance and skill.
Whose lives are bound in celebration. Who cook for the joy of
it. Who are honest and faithful and true to food. Who know
a good meal and cook it for you. Who try hard, live well, and
want to please. There are those we know. *Ittaikan!* And there
are others.

I chiban dashi

A red Spring haze hung over the drab kitchens of Shimura
Junior High School that morning; a trick of the light on the
school's old red brick which recalled for all of us who saw

it for the first time as freshers, in a bright little *eigakan* in Akanyio Bay, *E.T the Extraterrestrial*, in which an alien appears frighteningly in a young boy's cupboard and an ordinary child flies amazingly across a rainbow on a bicycle.

"That Spielberger!" Yuko cried out then, in the darkness. "He's got to be Japanese, or what?"

Now people were asking:

"So you think that famous *ninjo* saying about a person discovering the secrets of life in every great meal can come true at Mr Kishimoto's International Culinary Institute or what?"

"Respectfully," I said, in my fourteen-year-old voice, catching their drift, "you might laugh, yah. But, surely, yes, it can in our case."

Only then did they launch into their long discussions about the Kishimoto apprenticeship; about how it's from apprenticeships like Mr Kishimoto's that greatness has sometimes come about, but wars also. Success, but maybe also much destruction. Imagination but also, perhaps, some bad luck. Restraint but also, certainly, unseemly boasting. *Tarento*!

Interesting fact: many Japanese culinary institutes at that time, purporting to train great international chefs from the ages of 14 or 15, listed the following personality traits as absolutely essential to their young cookery graduates' success: confidence, patience, the ability to make "accurate and meaningful hand gestures", a willingness to greet people you may not otherwise like at all, and a "positive assertiveness."

"The thing is," I said, complete in my foreignness, "even if one of us knows we will suffer great shame during the apprenticeship . . . even if we knew *that*, we would go ahead and cook for Mr Kishimoto anyway. *Tomodaichi*, we can't help but cook."

"*Maa!*' people go on, "with greatest humility, *gaijin san*. Is it just possible that Kishimoto Shiro is mistaken from the start? Is not cooking about life, huh? About life-giving? About sustenance, not about . . . *schooling?*"

They say Mr Kishimoto risked much indeed in this culinary apprenticeship that pitted one young person against the next; that the Kishimoto Food Company's involvement in this apprenticeship did not contribute to the harmony of things, full as it was with expectation and that competitive spirit. Is it just possible that Mr Kishimoto's older brother, respectfully, should have taken more care with his inner family likewise? That, respectfully, the Kishimoto Company was known for its distinctive ways, its food marketing with no boundaries. Wasn't it the Kishimoto Food Company, after all, who sponsored all those national TV cookery-snookery shows, for example, that turned ordinary young cooks into guy-n-girl celebrities, that built those gastronomic malls that spread through bigger Japanese cities these days like monstrous seething sideshows, created those grinning chefs that are not real at all but look so real, living out their giant lives on those giant Kishimoto video screens like vengeful pixellated Gods harassing whole neighbourhoods of Japanese diners, them and those wise-cracking In-store Demonstration Kishimoto Company hosts. Hadn't the Kishimoto Food Company reduced cuisine in Japan to buffoonery and respectful family meals to dust?

I say: "*Sumimasen ga*. Okay. *Hai*, huh? Only, humbly, now let *me* tell *you* a thing or two about how I left junior high school to become a Japanese cook. . . ."

Yakimono

Yes, there are others, other Japanese cooks, Nobuko told me. And they had their place in Japan too. "To create havoc," she said, indirectly acknowledging my foreignness. In the worst

Japanese kitchens. In wicked kitchens. At the culinary home-plates of the criminal, the possessed, the evil, the bad. I stared at her in my occidental ignorance, my American ignorance.

Such evil kitchens stand as models of cruelty and shame. They reek of unhappiness and conceit. They attach themselves to the houses of good Japanese families like leeches and draw the lifeblood of entire neighbourhoods. They live at the rear of restaurants with the vindictiveness of a venomous snake hiding in the rockery of a playground. In these kitchens no one speaks. Nothing really good is ever made. The stench is atrocious. Like death warmed in an omelette maker, poached to a reeking fester. Like the carcass of some enormous pre-historical mammal, floored and cut open, spilling its billowing entrails into the humid atmosphere as volcanoes pop and squirt nearby. In these kitchens the very worst cooks we know make their play. The most evil, the criminal, the conceited and the just plain bad. They come from all kind of backgrounds, but they come with one purpose. To accumulate misery. To make Hell out of culinary substance. To taint good food with their horror and hatred, so that no meal is capable of unaffected warmth, no dish brings with it the surprise of the new or the unexpected delight. Nothing stands in the way of the limp and the indigestible, the bilious and burnt. Steam rills thick, brown and acrid here. There is a wash of opacity on the silver fronts. A drip of sauce on each old bottle. Waste accumulates in tubs bearing the faded markings of once used brands. *Shinodas Dripping. Narushima Fish-Oils. Grim-O-Remover.* These are the kitchens of the dispossessed. The kitchens of the ambitious but untalented. Here food is a trap. Here food is a curse. Here careers are made or broken. These kitchens are the razor's edge. The hot plate. The sharp end of the deal. Here new young cooks are made or broken. Innocence is lost or corrupted. The future is made bright or dark. These are the

kitchens of indecision and indetermination. The kitchens of
tako-rakugo. If you start your cooking career in one of these
Japanese kitchens, Nobuko says, you should hope you don't
end your career in one. You should fight like Heaven to break
out. You should draw on those internal resources that all new
chefs have, that impossible love affair with food. You should
cook like a *Karni*, like a diety, Nobuko says, like Alcide Mi-
robolant who, while Chef of his Highness the Duc de Boro-
dino, learnt to play piano better than Mozart simply so he
could coax out, with his sweet sound, the flavours of his *oeufs
à la Neige*. Or Alexis Soyer, Chef of the Reform Club from
1793 to 1825, who travelled from the English city of London
to the stinking farmers' markets of the Czech city of Prague,
by pony, to buy the very best lovage: the greenest, with the
yellowest of lumbels and its bitter skin removed. And he did
this each month. Yes, you should cook like you never cooked
before, or your life will end here, as an outsider in more ways
than one.

"*Choberigu* or *Choberiba*. One or the other. We can't be
both," Nobuko said. "We can't be good cooks having bad
days. It never ever happens. Good cooks never have bad days.
We can't be bad cooks acting good. It's impossible. People
can tell. Cooking doesn't work that way. You are either good
or you're bad. And, worst of all, you absolutely, completely,
can't choose."

Sushi

In total, six of Shimura's Junior High's students had been accepted to attend Mr Kishimoto's International Culinary Institute. I was the only non-Japanese. We had each received our
acceptance letters that morning from the Institute Registrar,
Mr Tieni Eiko. No Shimura graduates had been accepted for

entry in nearly 20 years; and now so many, and with a *gaijin* among them too! Because so many had been accepted, and because Mr Kishimoto was her uncle, Nobuko said she personally felt an obligation to now consider us, me included, as more than ordinary Japanese.

"Look at us!" she cried. "*Choberigu* huh? We are surely destined to be great cooks. Surely! From now on, *maa*, we're going to be *Chefanese*, Japanese combined with our undeniable destiny to cook."

The names of those Shimura students who were successful were posted on the noticeboard beside the principal's office: Four females: Kishimoto Nobuko, Kuroda Akio, Watasuki Yuko and Yonai Keiko. And two males: Saionji Masami and I.

"Now your uncle has made us Chefanese, Nobuko, we must all act the part," Watasuki Yuko said, as we stood in front of the board and each read over our acceptance letters from Mr Tieni, in which he set out the qualities for success at Mr Kishimoto's International Culinary Institute: individuality, perseverance, flair, attention to detail, determination and so on.

"*Hai!*' said Yonai Keiko, her hands flapping like butterflies. "It feels to me that our only real country from now on will be our kitchens and our cookery."

Standing in front of that noticeboard, I couldn't help dreaming about what we would do at Mr Kishimoto's International Culinary Institute. The others appeared to be doing the same.

"Maybe we'll learn to make *actual* Provencal Fish Soup," said Kuroda Akio.

"*Hai!* And those Yorkshire's whatsits," said Saionji Masami, ". . . *puddings!*"

"*Sumimasen ga!* How long since you seen your uncle, Nobi?" asked Akio.

"O," said Nobuko, now platting Akio's long hair into two fountain-like projections on top of her head. "I've never met him."

"How so?" I said.

"I don't know, yah. Until just lately, there'd been some bad words with my father and him. My father won't talk about it. I think, maybe, if they hadn't started talking again now, *maa*, dadsy wouldn't let me go at all."

"Phtt! And let you miss the opportunity to study with Kishimoto Shiro?" I said.

"Maybe just so, Koji." Koji, as they had christened me, after Koji Kondo, who had composed the music for the games *Super Mario Bros* and *The Legend of Zelda*.

"But hey!" said Masami. 'Think about what you wouldn't have learnt to do with a duck, yah!"

"And a shrimp," cried Yuko.

"And taro," cried Akio.

"And horseradish," cried Yuko.

On our way to our last History class we started to practice speaking in Cook.

"I hear finger buffets are very popular in New York City this year because the United States of American is becoming more informal," said Aiko, looking at me.

"*Hai!* But, in my view, two pork choices is certainly never enough for a modern *makunouchi* menu," replied Keiko.

"That thing between your father and uncle must have been some thing?" I said quietly, treading carefully.

"Hail to the grain mustard mousse," replied Nobuko, happy I think, but slightly apprehensive. "It's not a thing I know much about. Too young, yah."

Yuko broke in: "Natural gas is truly flip!"

"Sure," I said to Nobuko, "I get that. But now they're talking, yah?"

'Cookingly,' she said.

"O isn't that entirely gastronomic?" said Masami

"But, surely, a sea bass is a *choberigu* fish," said Kieko.

By the end of the day, all of us school friends were making Chefanese comments, unprovoked, in *kaiseki* places:

"Flash fry that," Yuko shouted out on the way home, office workers standing at stalls eating *anago*, lifting their tired eyes as they went on delicately skewering their food, maybe some *yaki-tofu* and rolled beef, scooping up *makunouchi* rice.

"Cappuccino sauces are really in," Masami told them, boldly.

"Why don't you prep that *right* now, huh?" I called, into a quiet crowd at a red-lantern stand.

"Just imagine a TV cooking competition, yah," said Keiko to us all, "where not one of the competitors actually says, when interviewed by a major international media celebrity, 'well, to be frankly frank, sir, my first love has always been classical French cuisine'. *Yerk!*"

We walked home along the streets of Akanyio Bay in our Chefanese utensil-print baggies, black beanies and white col-mar Chefanese coats, like we'd formed our own gastronomic *yakuza* gang. We made declarations about how after we had studied cookery with Nobuko's uncle we would all come to know most popular international ingredients simply by their scents. How we would be able to see menu plans in books of poetry and hear new dishes in chance rain showers. How we'd watch meals unfolding as if they were life plans and see the culinary experience in everyday things.

By Saturday we were due out at the Institute to enrol. Akio and Masami and Keiko and Yuko travelling out in a Kishimoto Food Company promotional van, while Nobuko and I, who had some business with our respected Sponsors, would fol-low later.

"Admit it, everyone," said Keiko, gathering her little hands to her cheeks as we reached the subway station, still clutching our acceptance letters in our hands. "How difficult is it anyway to fall in true love these days, huh? In heart-wrenching love, I mean. You know, that humming, singing love you used to fall in when you were no more than an infant? Love that knows no embarrassment and has no shame? Love that is as deep as our love of good cookery."

There in the subway carriage now, Masami tapping the carriage floor hard beside me with his shiny black plastic Chefanese boots, as we watched the Mclitter of the day slowly being kicked aside by the tramping mad evening crowd. All of us trying to put behind us our tiredness from the long semester so that we could share our speculations on what Mr Kishimoto's International Culinary Institute would actually be like.

"How incredible it is for us all to get into such an International Culinary School as your Uncle Shiro's, huh?" said Yuko, who was as lively as a bird. "No one cares about the art of cookery like we do, huh, Kishimoto Nobuko? Most cooks these days appear to be more entrepreneurs than they are artists."

"*Hai!*' I said, "most famous Japanese cooks you see on TV would rather sell you a t-shirt than cook you a meal in my view!"

"Respectfully, everyone,' said Nobuko. "And is *that* life?"

1

Miso-shiru

Departure day, and brightly colored flags, decorated with prints of fish and flowers from the week's local *kisetsu* festival, flapped in the light breeze around the modern homes of Akanyio Bay. Akio, Masami, Keiko and Yuko were leaving for Uncle Shiro's that morning. A deep green shiny curl entering the swathes of otherwise dull Spring grey alder leaves as if to wish them well, frilly like pork leg bunting, feathering around all the too quaint Akanyio Bay balconies, a heavy hint of white and pink cherry blossom on the trees. The Spring travelling season seemed to be in a particularly early swing, and well before the approaching Golden Week holiday too.

Nobuko and I, who had visited Shimura Junior High for the last time that morning, to collect our belongings, were walking home imagining no longer sitting on its polished mahogany benches, carving them with sequestered English words like "chowder" and "pimento" and "mirepoix", no more eating in its too-bright cafeteria or cooking in its sanitised Shimura Junior High Home Economy kitchens, no more separating: me to my Japanese class, her to her English class. We tripped down the road, scurrying past the curlicued school gates like red squirrels.

"Man, you can smell the future in the air like a waft of rye dough, huh!" cried Nobuko.

Coming in over the red-bricks of the school. Nestling there in the runnels between those too-quaint art nouveau turrets where Shimura had taught us a whole lifetime of innocuous classes from the tedious "Modern Economics II" to the pedantic "New Mathematics" and gave over a great part of its estate to cruel sounding wordplay: "*Examining* Chemistry", "*Exploring* Craft."

But, I knew, despite the shock that my own American parents expressed at my disregard of the traditional Japanese senior secondary school entrance exams, that we were about to progress beyond all this ordinary "examining" and "exploring." Finally, we were going to be *celebrating* cookery!

"The fact is," Nobuko said, calmly word-choosing, "they don't produce great cooks in most colleges any more, they produce *yatai* stall owners. *Sumimasen ga*. Those *choberiba* guys go off like egg gas bombs. My Uncle Shiro is different. You wait and see what happens, Koji. We'll eat all those Tōkyō University creeps alive."

"Gastronomic!" I said. "*Hai!* But, hey, what are we planning: the Hannibal Lecture of careers?"

"You're crazy, huh!" she said. "But no. Better."

"Better?"

"Cookingly better, Koji."

"Imagine," she said, "everything you ever desired could be eaten. I mean, not only food, Koji. Metaphorically speaking. Imagine, you know, that you can eat your way into some other, *better* life. That's what I mean about great cooks. They know who you want to be and they serve that dish up to you."

I watched all those too-dispassionate, too-career-tracked Tōdaibatsu-thinking Shimura Junior High freshers and their parents picnicking there on the grass in the late morning, just beyond the red brick fence, never in their wildest dreams prepping Rib-Eye Steak au Poivre or Baked Rigatoni with Mushrooms or Prosciutto and Cauliflower Tagine, and realised at that moment that, as far as Nobuko was concerned, none of them could ever possibly qualify like us to enter her uncle's International Culinary Institute.

It sounded as if one of them was playing a David Bowie song on some crude piece of hi-fi.

"Whatever happened to Bowie-san anyway?" said Nobuko, dreamily. "*Sumimasen ga.* But did he really turn into the world's first musical clothing-preneur, huh? Man, that is just too ripe! Imagine giving up on something just to sell things instead? Can a real pop musician simply do that, or a great TV actor turn into a full international furniture selling star, or a sportsperson win, what, the Nobel Peace Prize? Maybe Bowie-san will come back, huh Koji?"

"Fame is immutable, yah," I said, choosing "immutable" unfairly, given her English was so spectacular compared to my Japanese, yet still I wanted to prove something.

"Ain't that a fact?" she replied, unswervingly, and word-choosing I suspected, I return. "We don't have any choice anymore. Set menu, huh? Even bad Japanese cooks can get famous some way in the West now. And stay that way, huh, *forever*."

The transparent plastic cook's chest with your artificial heart beating slowly inside for everyone to see.

"Face it, Koji, successful cooks around here all have storefront hearts these days," Nobuko said. "Hearts with price tags. Most good Japanese *rakugo* end up being the homeboy short-orderers of mid-life Los Angeles mamas. The daughters every American father wants, huh? The clown prunes of this century's ethno food culture."

"But think," she said. "Think if at Uncle Shiro's we rub shoulders with *real* international chefs. Better cooks than

Keije Hidari and Sumie Mayuzumi. Much much better than Shohei Himeda and Yitsuko Sasaki and Hiroyuki Imamura. Better than Kuniko Kuga and Chishu Ozu and better than Yuharu Ryu. Real *kare raisu* haters, huh, Koji? Better even—what about!—than *Kyoko Kagawa?*"

"*Sumimasen ga . . .*"

"In fact, think if all that Kagawa could do was sit there watching us. Maybe eating one of those crazy artichoke hearts of hers, sizzling in one of her famous pomegranate flying saucers. How inspirational is that?"

"But you love Kyoko Kagawa!" I returned.

"Cookingly!" she cried, "but she must be, what, 45 years old, huh, a real old kamaboko-eating nana, and . . . What if I wanted to be better than that? Better than *Kagawa.*"

"*Sumimasen ga.* But maybe you're just suffering a bit from early May Syndrome, yah. What do you think?" I said.

"*Hai! Hai*, I don't think so."

I watched her twirling her hennaed hair around her fingers, the rings on her fingers catching the strands now and then and tugging at them. "You don't, huh?"

"Hey, what if I *do* want to be better than Kagawa ever was?" she said. "Better than every other one of those old terrestrial TV McChefs? Those restaurateur pseudo-chefs. Those entrepreneur un-cooks. Absolutely all of that TV McCookery. Those cooking teachers with their libraries of declarative, quaint-titled, total freaks' books: 'Hidari's Delightful Dozen', 'Kagawa's Naughty Nibbles', 'Sasaki's Gastronomic Greats'. Whatever. 'Soya-ya Confessional'. Is that stuff exploitative or what? *Yerk!* Uncle Shiro's Institute will have new cook teachers, I'm sure, ten times better than any of those."

And then there we would be, just Nobuko and I, Akio, Masami, Yuko and Keiko. Chefanese culinary geniuses.

Tamago-yuki

Over at the Kishimoto Food Company, where they were planning the first big food promotional event for some time, to accompany this year's cooks' apprenticeship program, Nobuko and I, Yuko, Masami, Keiko and Akio had respectfully become known lately as "The Hot Pots."

For most of our final junior high school year we had worked for Nobuko's father, Mr Kishimoto Yoshio, soon-to-retire President of the Kishmoto Food Company, as Kishimoto Food Company Hosts, demonstrating new food products in supermarkets and shopping malls and airports. The bright young Hot Pots! In the spirit of the renewed communication between the Kishimoto brothers, Nobuko's father had arranged for our applications to his brother's Institute to be sponsored by the companies we had represented as such hosts and on these scholarships we could afford, not least, to plan out our lives. Nobuko herself was sponsored by the Golden Valley Tea Company, myself and Akio by Big Boy Seafoods. Masami had secured the sponsorship of the Tanuki Sweets Corporation. Keiko of Hokkaidō Ice Supply and Yuko, much to our amusement, was to be sponsored by Taifū Beer Company.

"Big time Alcoholics Animus chef, huh, Yuko," we said, "what you cooking today, huh, beer-batter fishes?"

To make Yuko's situation worse, the office staff at the Kishimoto Food Company had named us all individually according to our sponsors. Myself and Akio as "Fish Chans", Nobuko as "Tea Girl", Masami as "Rice Cake", Keiko as "Ice Mountain" and Yuko, poor suffering Yuko, they had taken to calling "The Karaoke Kid." What cards! Only just teenagers, we had no restaurant yet to cook in. Not a physical one at least. But we knew we had already humbly tasted the commerce of cookery by being sponsored cookery hosts. Those demonstrations, the Kishimoto Food Company considered, were reaching the city's grassroots.

Ironically, in fact, since we were each recent students of the expensive Shimura school *and* Nobuko was the only daughter of the co-founder of that most "youth-conscious" of culinary names, and Japan's biggest food marketing company. For each of us there seemed to be floating all kinds of personal confluences in cookery: joy, desire, pain, passion, disappointment, happiness, determination, love, hate, laughter, song.

Is this life?

The great great writer Saikaku once remarked, following Voltaire my father notes, being a professor of literature, that cooking is life. He also praised the beauty of the sausage.

Tsumire

Yes, someone was singing, or strangling as it turned out that ancient Bowie anthem, *Rebel Rebel*. That said it all.

Now well after 7pm, the Kishimoto Food Company marketing tele-cast having dragged on as Okuma Masayuki, a recent vice-presidential promotion from Shin-Ekoda, wondered if there were not urgent matters to be discussed at Wednesday's board meeting and whether the *nemawashi* discussions had occurred to humbly allow this? Katsura Machiyo, a regional managing director who was flying in from Yamagata the next day, wondered also, and respectfully noted her thoughts that they might discuss how *Digitas Honshu* was a great channel on which to be selling food products this year (which frankly had no relevance at that point, but at least filled the dead webcast time with something like conversation) and Inuki Haruko, who was a senior executive director based in Kyoto, said, if he might express his feelings, that he was pretty sure that flights into Sapporo Intn'l Airport were running behind schedule at the moment due to problems with the automated scheduling or something and Masayuki then saying, out of the echoey, pixellated ether, that he thought from his recent travels that he noticed, with respect, an obvious prejudice across the country against those older style Kishimoto Food Company food promotions, and particularly the theatrical style of food marketing the Kishimoto Food Company still used in some areas, and that this, *domo, domo,* reflected a general lack of interest in such marketing strategies now, particularly among young people, and that Shochu Drinks Company, for example, which was producing some incredibly useful products, couldn't manage to boost their market share because of this, or Mr Benny's Soft Drinks, or Omu Crackers for that matter.

Nobuko's father, Kishimoto Yoshio, and his younger brother by three years, Kishimoto Shiro, built the Kishimoto Food Company on those lively old TV marketing campaigns of the 1960s and the company had specialised in food marketing ever since. They personally were the two guys who dressed up as desert spoons to put "Zest in Your Life with Zex" (the well-known American vitamin enriched shredded wheat) in 1964, and who literally stood naked in a tub of milk to munch away "Mom's Mondayitis" (with Saito's toffee buttons with extra sweetness) in '71. Together they invented that little tweeping toucan that hops from one popsicle to the next in that famous old *Twee Pops* TV commercial and "released" a whole flock of them onto those flat black TV screens during the Yamada trading turmoil of 1973, and they designed the glitter glow sets for *Aromalite*, the Italian coffee flavouring dispenser people. Those flickering studio backdrops all but launched Disco across Japan in the hot wet Summer of '75.

At that point, for some reason, the brothers had had some unfortunate words and decided to go their separate ways, Mr Kishomoto Yoshio continuing as president of the company and the younger Mr Kishimoto Shori, who remained a shareholder, opening his now famous cookery school.

When we had managed, some months back, to convince our parents to support our applications to Mr Kishimoto's International Culinary Institute, Nobuko's father, who had reached the *teinen*, the official age of stopping at the Kishimoto Food Company, and recently made up his differences with his estranged brother, agreed to ensure that our host companies would sponsor us, in conjunction with:

"The most considerable chef apprenticeship the Kishimoto Food Company has ever created," he said.

"At least," Nobuko said, "he doesn't want to *do* any of the promotions himself. *Sumimasen ga.* Him in a cock-a-doodle suit again! *Taihen desu!* Him singing "Leave My Heart in Kentucky" for the Liberty Dogfood Corporation. *Sheesh!* No. He just wants to be part of things."

The truth was, we fitted in at the new styled Kishimoto Food Company as uncomfortably as a pair of flat Kenji Yoda haute fashion heavy soled *setta* on the tiny feet of a *What's My Line* hostess. Certainly, unlike Nobuko's father, we were never, ever going to be big fans of Live In-Store Interviews and corny TV food jingles. In fact, our top three food hits were: Pizza home-del.. orange curd ice-cream and nameko mushrooms. In that order. Working at the Company had been good, but it was our dreaming about gaining entry into Mr Kishimoto's Institute that was uppermost in our minds.

We were going to be the swingingest, most up-to-the-minute Chefanesee in Japan, all the time listening to retro 20th Century music by big Western names like Beck and Ice Cube and R.E.M. Cooking up Svenska Köttbullar and watercress pancakes with saffron crab and farmhouse fruit pies and lazanki and brik à l'Oeuf and marble tea eggs with oriental mayo. Hanging out in all the upmarket *ryotei* just to watch the staff do their thing.

And yet, while we were all born too late to make much of the limping, flowery end of all that Pop-Art TV nostalgia that struck Japan while Nobuko and the others were at school (that is, with the broadcast of the AOTV's Christmas Special *John Lennon and His Beatles* in '00, which consisted, strangely, almost entirely of a long series of black and white photographs of members of *The Beatles* admiring Yoko Ono's Westernised butt), we all had a certain respect for Mr Kishimoto Yoshio's marketing style. What you might call "rehashed-Hippie." Nobuko was mostly relaxed about the subtle similarities between her father's way of doing things and our own—in her quieter moments she sometimes referred to these similarities as "The Kishimoto Family Trait", though not often—nevertheless, there was something else in us that wouldn't lie down and, as was inevitable, that something in our lives made itself heard in our unstoppable desire to discover all there was to know about cuisine.

Viva *Godzilla*! In us Chefanese the cooking monster lived. Now all we had to do was work suitably hard at Uncle Shiro's.

Sakana

"You think you make a foreign car Japanese by painting it yellow?" Nobuko joked, whispering sitting next to me in the back seat.

"Now you're crazy," I whispered back.

"*Domo*," she explained, "this is surely important, Koji. Yellow is the colour of digestion, yah? The colour of personal absorption?"

Her father pulled his little yellow Beemer up at the blinking orange lights outside the Matsuya store, and dropped us off. Nobuko and I looked so cookingly smooth.

Groups of Akanyio Bay school kids, with their brightly colored backpacks and little green caps, were sliding across the walk in long lines. Bunches of Japanese and Western tourists, who looked like they were expecting to find instant life-changing enlightenment in the oaken groves of Akanyio Bay, hovered on the street corner reading their free Tourist Authority maps, arms pointing every which way like Hong Kong Curry House mascots.

Many stores in the district had just started singing their *shaka*, which goes something like this:

O Bless Akanyio Bay boutique and craft district, humbly the fifth largest in Hokkaidō.

O Bless Akanyio Bay for housing this.

O Bless the wealthy for condescending to arrive every season to buy from the stores.

In fact, I had arranged that morning to go on my own to Nobuko's parents' place on Doi Shinkōkai Park, to thank her father formally for his support. "Absolutely, definitely *arranged* it," I said forlornly afterwards. I had even fortified myself somehow to listen respectfully to Nobuko's father's frequent mighty pronouncements on the current market for Chinese peanuts or the state of canned goods PR or the possibilities for some kind of new National Honey Manufacturers Association campaign this year. But when the lights changed and Nobuko left me behind to compose my thoughts, all I could manage to think was:

"*Oisogashi tokoro sumimasen*, Uncle Shiro, but who in Japan cooks for real anymore?"

Over and over again.

"Which famous Japanese *rakugo* really, *truly* cooks cuisine for real, huh?"

Until I couldn't manage to move at all.

"So much for a Shimura Junior High graduate confronting his destiny?" Nobuko said to me later, referring to the school principal's elaborate graduation speech.

Embarrassingly filled with self-importance, I so much wanted to do the "Look, Mr Kishimoto, no hands!" thing that morning. Had he seen, for example, our last few cookingly great Company promotions. And, if he had seen them, what did he think of our abilities—myself, and the others, that is, cooking for audiences, dressed up sometimes as the Steamed Sweet Hoy Op Crew, sometimes as Hangtown Fry American Vampires, sometimes as Steak House Sauciers or as the Janga Shrimp Gumbo Gang? All this part of the Kishimoto Food Company's distinctive style of youth marketing.

His own daughter, actually, was the most comfortable of us all in our million cooking host identities. Often I found it impossible not to think of Nobuko as the Hideko Takamine of supermarket hosting, experimentally swapping her own identify for something quite out of character, just as Takamine did as a cheap Tokyo stripper in Keisuke Kinoshita's great film *Karumen Kokyo Ni Kaeuru*. That morning, however, she was quiet and reflective and tense. We hadn't heard for hours from Akio, Masami, Yuko and Keiko, who were supposed to be in a Kishimoto Food Company promotional van, on their way to Uncle Shiro's international culinary institute in Naorai and, quite frankly, it was concerning us considerably.

"Please hold. Your call is entirely invaluable to us here" followed by the line abruptly dropping out. Their service kept coming up with these automated excuses: "With considerable respect, you have selected an invalid extension. Do please deem to dial again."

If that wasn't bad enough, the student hall where we were all supposed to be staying in her Uncle Shiro's wasn't answering either. It was as if the world's entire population of Chefanese had dropped into the dark meandering waters of the Na-orai District, and we felt entirely responsible for it. Our own private food hosts' nightmare! That night Nobuko's father had arranged for us to be thirty miles away in Miyagi at a little *ryo-tei* called *Essay in Idleness* to meet Nobuko's second cousin, Hi-ra—a still young cook who had also been accepted to attend Uncle Shiro's Institute and who, Mr Kishimoto had reported, as he encouraged us to introduce ourselves to him, was un-equivocally laudable with umeboshi and flavoured daikon.

On Macaque Avenue, way up past the Middle East Café and the Shobo Bookshop, up past the Kathmandu *nomiya* and Ko-bo's Used Clothes, cute pairs of brand new Shimura High freshers with their deep blue Shimura neckerchiefs right up tight on their throats were buying Haagen-Dazs with their parents at the Green Parrot Creamery, vying for the single set of outdoor tables and watching the punks, or post punks, who were emulating the New York punk movement, which had itself come out of a retro thing in Japan for that British punk movement of the late 1970s, which emerged out of the electric guitar movement that struck, and ultimately split, the American folk movement of the 1960s, simultaneously kill-ing off Japan's growing interest in Western traditional instru-ments, while fuelling the country's electric guitar explosion. Many young people believed Bob Dylan had a lot to answer for in Japan.

These post punks were mixing with some Hip-Hop kids and some girls who seemed to be pretty much into Death Metal and some R&B soul sisters and a bunch of Nelly Furta-do fans (at least, they had her t-shirts) and they were stand-ing over on the stone wall, one of them every now and then jumping up and sliding a skateboard along the wall edge until one of the soul sisters stepped down into the little amphithe-atre where sometimes cookware companies did displays and local firemen performed acrobatic tricks on top of bamboo ladders and suggested they all go and get coffee at *Douters*. And so, beating their fire-sticks on the sidewalk in a kind of African hunting rhythm, they set off in the direction of Akanyio Bay Herbarium and the noodle bar district that spread out around there.

Pausing there at the door of the Shobo Bookshop I thought those Hip-Hopping girls looked alarmingly beautiful, like any one of a dozen well-known *gegika* cartoon characters, one of those stunning Akira home-girls who decorate three-quarters of the food districts of every city these days, way up on electronic billboards, stamping their pointed black digitised boots on the pavement of some purple bulb noodle world, DV projected onto the sides of office buildings, chiselled out of the features of a Westernized Japan like some cute thing Walt Disney had done with a wild boar. As I told the others that night, after consuming two promotional cocktails straight from their faux-poco glasses—which might explain things— that I had been thinking about going in to the bookshop and buying a copy of Sano Toshiko's new book "Cooking Disasters that Truly Have Worked."

"*Yomiuri Shmibun* is calling it a real domestic event," I said, my face lowering into my hands, speaking through cracked lips, my eyes almost welded shut, hair tugged into ugly fat wads.

Apparently the book was constructed around several completely ruined Western meals, something like volcanic eruptions from which an orchids grow or earthquakes in whose aftermath hundreds of lost babies are found happily alive: stromboli in which the dough goes moist and takes on the shape of the provolone within, a *besugo a la parrilla* in which you inadvertently have used a silver bream instead of a red and the texture is therefore too coarse, rough even, like a deep-sea fisherman's potluck pie, a tomatillo salsa that is barky and too crisp, and so on. Through which Sano builds up such a philosophy, such a powerful argument for the sheer subversiveness of cooking Western food in Japan, comparing, as she does, the curdling of a horseradish cream with the Fall of Rome, the taste of a dwarf leek to the sensation of your first kiss and the sight of a badly shaved white truffle with a sunset partially obscured by the flat black glass of the STC Intercommunications Centre that, by the end, you long for something to go wrong in your next batch of *crepes parmentier*, for something to turn your walnut sauce into a bitter landfill of browned double-cream, or to brutally sour your ossbucchi nuts. Very very Kagawa.

But, despite the nervousness I was feeling about the apprenticeship I couldn't quite bring myself to go into Shobo and buy the Sano book.

"I simply couldn't let another TV cookery-chookery into my life at this point," I told everyone, "what with our *kao* on the line like this."

Instead, I hovered at the old bookshop window, surveying that Shobo desertscape of "Recommended Textbooks" and "New-Releases" and "New DVD-ROM Titles" until one display simply washed its way into the graphic glitter of another and I began carefully to cook, at least in my mind, something simple and fresh, just to clear my head: a tomatillo salsa, finely chopped; sautéed scallops on a bed of Parmesan polenta; some Tibetan *shaptak*; lobster *feuillete*; Demerara wafers; glazed shallots; Chantilly potatoes with a Yoghurt crust. Each additional step, of course, would bring me closer to Nobuko's parents' house. Bulgar and Fava Bean Soup. Closer to her father's marketing declarations. Cod with Corncob Broth and Gingered Eggplant. Her father's sometimes disapproving clicking of his tongue on the roof of his mouth, signalling his disinterest. Cherrystone Clam Serviche. . .

Moving off, an old woman in one of Shimura Junor High School's grey ancillary staff uniforms suddenly appeared in the window next to me, hobbling at my pace.

"*Sumimasen ga!* Excuse me, greatly," she barked, "but where might you be headin'?" matching my cooking-induced stroll with a slow grandmotherly shuffle of her own. An old Filipino Shimura Junior High cleaner woman with a flock of seagulls do and a kind of knitted black hat, which had a name for it but I couldn't remember what. Rude as she was, I tried to resist answering, but finally, the old woman keeping pace in a kind of awkward dance, I shot back:

"Nowhere."

The old woman, not even turning, frog marched that. "*Kora!* Looks like somewhere to me, un?"

"No way she was big," I said, with embarrassment, to Nobuko, Akio, Masami, Yuko and Keiko afterwards, "but she was sure rough and as tough as, you know, twine?" She made me think that maybe she was a den mother or something. A den mother for maybe ten inter-connected Filipino families somewhere over in the poorer areas of the district of Tama, I thought, where cooking is genuinely *gaijin ryōri yō no. Crabe Farcies, Berehein na Forno, Callaloo* and the like.

"*Hai!* Chickadee going as fast as youse going gotta be going some place," said the old woman.

"Look," I shot, propping before the window of a pachinko parlour, on the edge of the shopping district, near Akanyio Bay's Electric Energy Museum, "old woman, you hearing me? *No* money!'

"Respectfully," said the old woman, bright and as forward as an electric button. "But that's not how it looks to me."

I realised I was still wearing our Company uniform from attending that afternoon's meeting, and immediately reeled back against the window. We tended to dress up Chefanese when we were at Nobuko's father's offices, so that we wouldn't blend in with all those young persons at the Kishimoto Food Company in Yamamoto suits and Etam black calf-high boots, the Kawabuko V-Necked cotton sweaters and Hot Ocean Surfwear Slash-necked viscous tops. Of course, I didn't blend in so well anyway.

You know the joke: "How many Hot Ocean Surfwear slash-necked red tops does it take these days to build a career in a Japanese corporation?"

Three.

Why?

No reason.

Sometimes we wore t-shirts from food companies like Sō, who locally made Tweakies Suckers and Brimore, who manufactured the Cool Crunch range of breakfast cereals, Cool Orange Crunch, Cool Farm Crunch, Cool Choco Crunch and the like, and Han's who made not Chinese produce but saltines. Nobuko said all of the Kishimoto Food Company office used to be like that back in the 1970s and 1980s. Crazy promo teams, guys in chicken suits and Robert Palmer t-shirts and "I Love New Coke" hats and so on. But not now. Now it was Tony Hitfinger suits and Nickol Farty blouses and all those ads with *omamori* in them. All that "Genuine *Makunouchi Bento* Box' branding and Takje Sanoyka stuff. *Yerk!* So there I was in my Chefanese utensil-print baggies, black beanie and white colmar Chefanese coat.

Interesting fact: even in what you might call "this day and age", Japanese food marketers, seeing themselves cast on the web, continue to think of themselves largely as TV stars. Go figure.

"Okay. Okay," I said, reaching into my coat pocket. "I'm going to *give* you some money. You can go and buy . . . *food*. Food? Is that what you need?"

"Child," said the old woman, "is it possible you have some big attitude?"

"What?" Whispering loudly. I could hear an unfamiliar shudder in my voice. "*Twa!* My attitude! Mine! . . . I say I am going to give you money. I don't actually say what you must do with it. I'm going to give money to you to buy your . . . *food*. Compute, huh?"

"I didn't actually think that the old woman was going buy, food, yah?" I said some time later, when telling this story. "I figured, obviously, maybe some *choberbi* Cambodian hashish. *Hai!* Maybe something like a clean *yukata* might have been good, huh."

"Oo," said the old woman, loudly. "Don't want it. Don't want 'food', respectfully. Food? *Yah!* I got *food*. Just want to walk with you, kid."

The old cleaner set off.

Stopped when she realised I wasn't following.

Came back.

"*What?*" I shot, straight at her.

"*Hora!* You *ain't* listenin'," said the old cleaner. "I don't want food, *oya*. Just walk with me, kid."

"No," I said, abrupt now. "I don't want to walk with you. A-Okay, huh? . . . crazy woman."

"Crazy woman?" said the old woman. "*Kuso!* Walk with me."

She unashamedly grabbed my arm, and before I had actually agreed to it I was walking along with her. Striding more like it. First across Daibutsu Square, and then onto Yachigusa Street. Me at such a pace that I could hear the rude old woman's breath shallowing and imagine the hard, tight worming in her chest. Her arm felt like a loop of wire through the left side of my body.

The whole thing reminded me a little of that time, a month earlier, when Nobuko's father had taken all us Kishimoto food hosts to Niseko to try *Pichones con Salsa de Camarones.*

"The best South American food in Japan," Mr Kishimoto had said; but Nobuko fell ill afterwards and we spent three days visiting a little mountain ski hospital watching Nobuko having her stomach periodically vacuumed by a local team of mad men and even madder women until her sides looked like they'd been badly brunoised by a guy from *Hideo's All-You-Can-Eat Italian Pizzeria.*

Rumour was the young Peruvian *gaijin* had mistakenly taken his pigeons from the streets of Niseko, in and about the filthy old *gassho-zukuri* houses all braced and bound with their rotting straw rope. The guy was cooking with diseased birds; but that didn't change how Nobuko felt: she said she would have eaten it anyway.

"Don't worry, dadsy," she said, from her hospital bed, "frankly, it's not a taste I'd be prepared never to have."

"So where you from?" asked the old cleaner woman.

If I could have pulled back an answer by that time I would have done it, but I could ever hide myself away like that from such abruptness. I was like a book left open in a bookshop, a newspaper some mid-salaried underwriter is absorbed in reading on a crowded subway train.

"No lying?" the old woman said, when I said I lived in Akanyio Bay, which, to all intents butts the new housing district of Tama like an orchid blooming on a pile of steaming cow dung. The old woman craned her small round head to look right into what Masami has called my "willowy face", staring for what seemed like a full minute, more, and then breaking into a tiny, round-toothed grin.

"*Hai!* The Bay? . . . Little boy. *Me too.*"

The impossibility of that hung in the air like a genuine local sighting of Elvis Presley.

Onto Ukiyo-e Street now, crossing Kagura, cooking in my mind a Southern American clambake, the apartments giving way to houses, all that suburban shiplap and old world wisteria and plaques with Japanese translations of bright little Western names like "The Elms" and "Rose Cottage" and "Mr Bronson's."

"I was brought up over in Akanyio Bay,' I continued, remembering in a half-hazy moment my parents' first big Japanese apartment on Jakachu Square with its hardwood floors and its damp parking underneath and the Tama Waterlands over yonder, that everyone was talking about cleaning up with those mounds of tax money rolling into the Akanyio Bay Big Excavation around that time, I found out later; and which, eventually, became the tenement estate of Tama itself. I was only five years of age, and newly arrived from Boston. Akanyio Bay was still pretty much the biggest *nouveau-riche* development area in the city at that stage.

"*Hai!*" said the old woman. "Akanyio Bay, huh? No lying, yah? . . . Me too."

Interesting fact: the most popular names for international restaurants contain a word relating to the concept of "home"—as in Aberdeen Steak House, Palm Cottage or The Green Olive Hut. Does this mean, maybe, that most people view these restaurants as extensions of their own family environments and therefore can be expected to react to their cooking with the same variety of intense personal responses indicative of peoples' feelings toward their relatives?

The old woman's black eyes kept a perfect beat with the pumping movements of my hands. To and fro, watching me and the roadway behind and the pathway ahead in a kind of scheduled patrol. Rhythmic. A movement I couldn't grasp, especially in one so old. I realised now that I was going to get to Nobuko's parents' house a millennium too early, certainly before her father arrived and that, even though Akio, Masami, Yuko, Keiko and I sometimes had trouble with his *un-ojisan* exurbrance, this meant facing Nobuko's mother alone.

We had not seen Nobuko's mother for weeks and she would want me to tell her whether Nobuko was going to invite her to come to the welcoming party at her brother-in-law's cookery school and Nobuko was not sure whether she could cope with having her mother there and therefore I would not be able to answer and this would be a difficult, in fact an almost impossible situation to be in.

It had been barely five months since Nobuko had driven us all out one Saturday morning to Naorai Island and shown us her uncle's International Culinary Institute, perched there regally on the waters' edge with its spires and turrets, and said that her father had said if she was determined enough about this "cheffery-peckery" of hers to be accepted into his brother's Institute he would arrange for our sponsors to ensure all of those working for the Kishimoto Food Company would be properly supported, and that he would highlight this client sponsorship with a giant Food Festival during his brother's annual apprenticeship competition.

It seemed to me, respectfully, that Nobuko's father was not taking too well to the idea of retiring from his company and that he thought the high profile apprenticeship might be something he could do, perhaps even in direct provocation of the Kishimoto Food Company's new, bright corporate plans, which were largely to weed out the style of pantomime advertising Mr Kishimoto and his brother had been doing in the 1960s, 1970s and 1970s—celebrity challenges, sportspersons with brands tattooed on their rumps, eating marathons, talking animals, skywriting campaigns, movie-star impersonators, manga comic ads, pop-music-athons—and replace it with something they considered much more refined. I could see the Kishimoto Food Company's headquarters, clinging in white stuccoed balconies as he spoke, like perfectly manicured fingernails to the bay edge, almost twenty miles across the dark water to the west.

"This year's Kishimoto apprenticeships will be the relaunch of the adventurous Kishimoto," he told us, secretly in a popular *akachochin* near Company's offices, knowing that the whole plan he was hatching went against the very idea that the only thing a retiring president was supposed to do was to keep the younger account executives informed about the traditions of the company.

"*Hai!* It'll be the Kishimoto again, huh, that Shiro and I founded?" he said. "Who knows, we might even make the new Kishimoto Food fun, yah?"

His campaign at the launch of this year's apprenticeships was going to be, in every way, Mr Kishimoto's defiant act of self-definition. These were his bold parting words to us:

"So tell me truly then, *kodomo-tachi*, does or does not a Japanese chef have to cook only for duty and to put food on the table these days? Cannot he also still cook for glory?"

Self-possessed, some salarymen might call it. Self-satisfied. But Nobuko's father had genuine needs and they were not so far removed from our own. For one thing, though we hadn't the words to describe it, we each blamed ourselves for our parents' successful lives. We were silently thinking in our fourteen-year-old way that we were just amalgams of their ordinary middle class Japanese values, even me, founded on that great rush of wealth that came into Akanyio Bay at the opening of the twenty-first century. "We're like drone bees, yah" we told each other just a few years later, "living out one

day after the next in perfect, stupid honey-buzzing happiness."
We didn't realize that drone bees are production line workers; that the only bee we would really understand, in human
terms, as having a choice of the menu we had was The Queen.
Though we always thought of ourselves as far in advance of
those formulaic Shimura graduates we each silently believed
that our Akanyio Bay upbringing threatened to make our own
cooking uninspired, for one thing, and our future lives a kind
of simulation of every other good life, for another.

"We've just never had any real thing to deal with," Nobuko
once said over lunch at *Whiskey Purple*. "That's the fact of it,
yah. It's like when you wake up each and every day and it is
always so gloriously, unfailingly flip. You know? Every day.
One after another. Forever! I mean, what kind of life is that?"

"*Hai!* What kind?"

We thought of our acceptance of the offer to train in Uncle
Shiro's apprenticeship program as a chance to sail the dark
waters of human suffering. To smell the scent of raw ambi-
tions. To feel the texture of unfulfilled desire. So it went. And
being part of the Kishimoto Food Company's campaign at Mr
Kishimoto's International Culinary Institute could only add
to the honor should one of us actually be accepted to join the
Food Company as a fully trained chef.

Kuri-no-ama-ni

"Did you ever see that corny 1980s TV show called *Fantasy
Island*?" Nobuko said.

"Sure," I said. She sometimes asked me about Western
things without thinking about what it meant for her to do so.

Starring Ricardo Montalban as Mr Roarke, an island resort manager, and Herve Villechaize as his diminutive assistant, Tattoo.

"*Sumimasen ga*, when I was a kid," she said. "I fell totally in
love with Mr Tattoo.'

Made sense: Tattoo and Nobuko were the same size then, after all, and Tattoo's playboy ethic was right down a wealthy Akanyio Bay kid's alley.

The premise of this popular American show was this: that a single visit to Fantasy Island, flying in by seaplane as it turned out, and immersion in just one of your dreams, which Mr Roarke would recreate for you according to his own enigmatic interpretation, would change your life forever. Very 1980s, I guess. Montalban with his white suit and coiffure barnet. The smiling holiday Freudian. Villechaize, no taller than a six year old, and dressed to match in a Hilton Hotel chain silver service waiter's white monkey suit. You could have been mistaken for thinking they were father and impish son.

"De plane! De plane!" squeaked Villechaize, Montalban cocking his dentured jowl.

And down it would come, the whirring plane up to the rocking wharf. Hawaiian-Japanese looking lap girls draping the confused Fantastists with leis. The grass hotel. Fortuitous meetings in the jungle. Lost lovers. Mighty volcanoes. Childhood illnesses. Rocky career paths. The whole lot spewed out like your innards along the sea grass pathways of the island, around its quiet green waterfalls. Guests included cameos from some well-known Hollywood film stars in decline, such as Ann-Margaret and Robert Stack. Bill Bixby and Victoria Principal, who would both go on to fame shortly afterwards in *The Magician* and *Dallas* respectively, significantly starred in the TV pilot.

This was our Chefanese blueprint. Our arrival at Mr Kishimoto's International Culinary Institute was going to be our *Fantasy Island*.

Utō Street was narrowing as it approached the river. The old shiplap industry captains' houses were larger and further back from the roadway and the cars sparser on the kerb, drives leading back to the houses protected by great stands of she-oak and beech and cherry and hickory.

"O yeah," the old cleaner woman was saying, 'youse grew up in Akanyio Bay, I was born in Akanyio Bay. *Tatamae*, you and I. We're Akanyio Bay *hitobito*, yah?"

This Akanyio Bay thing seemed bizarre enough, I thought, given how every family there knew every other family's business in the Bay. There were no mad old aunts in Akanyio Bay. At least none that were allowed to continue to live at home. But maybe mad old aunts would not be out of place for residents in Tama. Perhaps not in Kampyo. But Akanyio Bay was like a purse of pure, distilled hum-drum, a big 21st Century theme park for executive central managers and foreign company vice-presidents who thought plexi-glass was beautiful at sunset and Japanese women in lambs-wool sweaters were obviously playing the field.

"You Buffalo fan, huh?"

The Kintetsu Buffaloes. Baseball?

"Kind of," I said. Why, I was wondering, do old *gaijin* working women's conversations spiral so determinedly in on themselves when they meet other *gaijin*. It was as if they were idiomatically imploding. Maybe, I thought, that explained why you never saw many of the Shimura Junior High auxiliary staff on the street. Rather than being in their street clothes, and therefore in disguise, they were in fact disappearing verbally into themselves, swirling around in their own unfathomable word worlds until they slid back through the cracks of suburbs like Tama, back to their widescreen TVs.

"*Domo*, kind of, huh?" said the old woman, elongating the "of" into a pursed, oval non-Japanese projection *awwf*. "Kine *awwf*. I thought so. Me too, yah?"

Interesting fact: a newspaper report recently in *Shonen Jump* announced that the winners of this year's International Restaurant of the Year Awards include Iola (Best Interior Design), Schlick (Best Bargain Meal), The Real Bean (Best New Restaurant), Mama Mia (Best Family Restaurant), The Duke of Bedfordshire (Best Gastropub) and Tarka (Best Vegetarian Meal). None of these restaurants serves Scandanavian food. None provides a text-message booking service. None offers the option of a private room. None has a speciality coffee selection. Maybe this says something important about the nature of the culinary experience.

"Great," I said.

"Great," said the old woman. *Graay-ta*. "Kind *awwf* a fan. You like that Isao Senda?"

"Me," she said. "I sure like Isao. He's got some right arm, huh? . . . I like Jerzy Zebrowski. . . . Big *gaijin*, huh?"

"He is a very big hitter," I said carefully, though my knowledge of baseball was not as good as it should have been, "like Zebrowski"

"You freaky little creep," suddenly hissed the old woman, and before I could wonder what, or where this had come from, I was bunted hard. From the side. Into a jungle of damp domestic shrubbery. Onto the shaded wet ground. And completely out of sight.

Down in the rhodora and sweet fern, the old woman's elbow down hard on my head, my face being squashed into the nutty leaf-litter, the wiry old cleaner woman's hands scooting around me in the undergrowth like a ferret, the smells of cats and suburban rot forced up hard against my nostrils, it occurred to me that if I lived through this I would find it hard even to mention it to anyone, and certainly could not mention it to Nobuko's father. It would seem like an impossible event, some out-of-body experience that would only declare me different from everything a student accepted into the Mr Kishi-moto's International Culinary Institute stood for. "You know," I was bizarrely thinking, "out of a crayfish comes a pot au feu. From a goose comes a Ballotine of goose with Savigny-lès-Beaune. In an ordinary melon lies the basis of a Corsican Salad with Pork and Melon. This almost certainly would never happen to Mr Suburban Awayuki Party."

"Give me your pocketbook!" hissed the old woman. Snaking her right hand over me now, eyes clocking one way and the other like town clocks, her left hand pressing my face down into the mud. "Hurry up."

Trying to get my hand down inside my jeans' pocket, cranking my arm up from under her hefty arm and offering up my wallet. Like a canary I just rescued from a laundry woman's cat, I would think later. Quivering there in my outstretched hand.

"Freaky little *gaijin kogaru* prince," the old woman growled, snatching the bird.

Though her arm suddenly lifted from my head, I kept my cheek down hard in the mud.

"Zebrowski," the old woman snarled at me, and spat long and stringy on the ground beside me. "He got no right arm, little royal princey. He just some rich import creep. Dig?"

And then, just as quickly as she had appeared, the old woman was gone.

2

Buri teriyaki

Despite our young selves we all really did love Kyoto Kagawa. Because, I guess, she was as humbly close to the perfect Chefanese as we could imagine before we ourselves were properly trained. She was almost complete. You had to admire her near-completeness. She was every Japanese cook's ideal *obasan*. She was the Goddess of Domesticity. She had even written a book of the same name. *I am the Home Goddess*. Had everyone read that book? Had they absorbed the sheer audacious brilliance of it? It was like a rock thrown in the stagnant pool of professional cookery. A jewel in the rock garden of modern Japanese food writing. We envied *and* admired her. So much that Yuko joked now and then about how we might one day have to kill her, only because her living at all was completely incredible. She was a creature impossible enough to invent that sometimes it felt like she might not actually exist. The Queen of Queensine. The Self-taught Gopher of Gastronomy. An impossible impresario. An improvising imp. We watched her like hawks. We thought all her shows were in some manner historically great. In our imaginations we had modelled our not yet started careers after hers. Yes, we thereby dedicated ourselves respectfully to your *sabi*, Kagawa. See how I can lift the sauté pan in a casual shake? See Masami's kitchen scissors snapping away at fresh wakame?

Man, it's madness - but it's you. See the unsalted butter, the good pancetta, the Springform tins, the fresh berries, the robust rice wine, the horseradish-fromage-frais, the New York chocolate buttons. That is you. That was her. She was our role model. After everything, after all that has happened since then I wonder, had Kagawa warned me, might things have turned out differently?

Ika

As I came up on the *engawa* of Nobuko's parent's house I was still feeling as if I'd been mauled. A poor *rakugo* spat from the foul, taste-saturated mouth of modern society I was thinking, in my 14 year old way.

"*Sumimasen ga.* So now we have *choberiba* crime in the *sakara* suburbs, huh," I kept repeating, mantra-like. Kind of weirdly detached, frankly. "This is *it*. Wealth motivated crime now in Akanyio Bay."

It was making what you might call the culinary "hole" in me deeper I believe, just to think about that, Akanyio Bay being the kind of place that had long had success in banishing the worst aspects of the modern city from it and replacing it with such a neat, round version of contemporary Japanese life that you got used to its completion and comfort and forgot anything elsewhere existed, ever. "If Kagawa was born anywhere in the suburbs," we would often say, "then certainly it would be here." If international cuisine has a domestic style then Akanyio Bay has created the evolution of that style. It is the mushroom ragout of suburbs. The lentil and chestnut soup of suburbs. The hazelnut and raisin bread of suburbs. It has the lowest inner-city crime rate in the North-East, and the highest number of police officers per head. Somewhere I read once that Akanyio Bay has more police officers per head than almost all the key financial centres of the world, except for Hong Kong, which has a large and visible *omawari* for tourism reasons as much as anything. But in Akanyio Bay tourism is hardly a giant industry, the tea-shops and reports that the philosopher and bon vivant Daisetz Suzuki once "took tea" out here only taking people so far, and the usual motives for visiting are more corporate and clever, centred around the white-collar hi-tech industries on east side of the river and the banking and insurance head offices around Zojoji and Nenjago and Dekura Streets on the west.

I was weighed down by Akanyio Bay's heritage, and by my own foreign one, at that moment. I heard Nobuko's mother's voice in my head, adding to the tautness, asking things like:

"Did the old woman have a smell?"

and

"How exactly did she disappear? Were there any signs of burning?"

Interesting fact: the average length of training for a good sous chef is four years. However, sous chefs working in the late nineteenth century at the *L-Aventure* restaurant in Lyon, France, spent four years alone practising *salmis de palombe*. Some never progressed beyond this. Go figure.

"A *hashi*," Nobuko's mother would probably call the attack, meaning it was a bridge occurrence, something which came from the edge of experience between the material and the spiritual worlds. Evil in this case. Or that it was the action of some caring *Bodhisattva*, or Enlightened Being, who knew more about my condition than I myself knew at the time, and that it was bound to be connected, her mother would say, with my failure to fully realise my potential.

And then there would be talk of asking one of my relatives, most of whom I rarely saw and, I secretly believed, probably didn't exist. Phantom American uncles and make-believe aunts that my parents used to tell people about in order to maintain their own sense of family. The only two that had appeared, anytime, ever, in my childhood were an Uncle Ned and an Aunt Kate, though Ned in fact worked in the Head Office of NES Corporation, over in Sapporo, and was more into Folding Files and PDA accessories than poltergeists; and Kate, who was four times divorced, knew as much about spirituality as the guy who delivered the crab haul, having taken her fourth (bio-tech investor) husband to the cleaners in order to keep herself in package holidays to Australia's Great Barrier Reef, to which she had in recent years become almost entirely addicted.

At the beginning of my final year in junior high, when Nobuko and Yuko, Masami and Akio and Keiko and I were deciding not to sit the senior high school entrance exams, my mother had persuaded my father, by reference to his literary interests (Comments such as "He'll visit rue Jean-Dolent, where Cendrars did his best work", and the like) to pay for me to spend a semester in Europe studying at the Salon Culinaire de Roux in Genoa, under Mr Jacobo Tatti, but I had stayed two weeks and, discovering Mr Tatti was not all he had claimed to be, asked to return apologetically to school. That, in itself, was evidence enough for my father.

"What is it you imagine you are going to do at Mr Kishimoto's Institute?" my father asked me, when I announced that I preferred not to sit the senior high school exams after all, with his permission.

"*Istumo osewani natte orimasu,*" I said, "a career", keeping my mother in sight, out through the sliding doors, sitting in the small family garden of our Akanyio Bay house.

"In cooking?" asked my father, speaking out through the kitchen window toward my mother and the bay beyond.

"Respectfully," I said, adopting Japanese reverence if not my Japanese language, "not only." Because I imagined my cookery would be so much more than a career: a gathering of unsettled minds, a convergence point of tastes and personal techniques, a clash of Titans, a sporting event, an art exhibition, a sleep-over, a party, a club, a raw nerve, a trial, an epiphany.

My, mother, like Nobuko's, kept drawings of food products on the walls of the home in silver frames. Never manufactured popcorn portion packs. Tinned products. Frozen goods. She and Nobuko's mother had been product designers at Nakasone Foods in the late 1980s, two of what some people still called the "Nakasone Dream Team" who had thought up the Salt-free Beef Cube and the Sugar Bead. Two Shikoko Island girls, my mother the daughter of a US naval captain stationed there, Nobuko's mother the daughter of a wealthy local building contractor, each with a flair for artistry and a head for food products. In the early 1980s, my mother said Nobuko's mother, Mita Mikko, had been unarguably the most brilliant of food product designers in the industry. They had both resigned from their jobs soon after. My mother to marry my professor father, who she met at a Hitoshi Nomura exhibition, and Mita Mikko to marry crazy food marketing genius Mr Kishimoto Yoshio, who was twenty-five years her senior.

My mom would sometimes ask if I had heard from Jacobo Tatti and I would say, embarrassed to tell her more, that I hadn't. She wrote to him sometimes. My mother wrote to Jacobo Tatti giving him the latest on his protégés plans and inviting him to visit her home for Heaven's sake! She asked Jacobo Tatti if maybe he would come to Japan and talk to her American son about his abandonment of his studies abroad. Thankfully he never replied.

Yakitori

The Kishimoto family home on Ikasama Park looked like an ice sculpture, part Japanese, part a reference to the American, from what I recalled of the architecture of America. Something a northern *Ainu* maybe in thick green ice-sculpting goggles would swoon over, carving out its slate blue stucco from a slab of Indigo tinted ice in the dining room of the Kyoto Meridian Hotel, hoving out its white windows, giving it the appearance of something literally living, two pointed ears in the place of its turrets, two wide eyes in the place of its front windows. Gasping and groaning there.

As a child of maybe eight or nine I'd seen talented Japanese ice sculptors in big hotels in Sapporo carve ice into the enormous Buddhas. Once, in a tourist *kaiseki* place where my parents and I were staying, out near the lake at Ishikari, a kid not much older than me made an entire Himeji Castle out of a block of ice the size of a fridge-freezer. We have been taught that ice sculpting is still one of the most underrated culinary arts.

The Kishimoto family home was one of those High Yatoi places, showing that imported New England influence, all tile mantels and Chifforobes. The *engawa* and porches were a half a dozen people wide and, at that time of year, the wisteria grew up over its trellises like engorged purple veins. On the drive side, down toward the garage where Nobuko's father kept each new model of Chrysler, I could make out the long rear Western porch, up high on its stone pillars, and a netball hoop on the corner for the girl that once lived here. But Nobuko was only 5'3; she never could shoot that hoop.

Then I was up on the stone steps and removing my shoes.

Interesting fact: commercial Japanese honeys are usually clover honeys, though few honey manufacturers admit they

are limited to these; often they will color their honeys to suggest they are more varietous than they are. Sometimes a small-
er, boutique company in Kyūshū might sell a genuine lavender
honey, but the quality is usually poor as lavender honeys are
dependent on warm weather for their flavour and most fields
of lavender, even in Kyūshū, grow in cool or temperate zones.
There are, of course, other honeys. The cicely, which is spicy
and sharp, is well known in parts of Eastern Tôhoku. And
the lemon grass, which is bitter, but soft on the tongue, and
common on the Indian sub-continent. But the real champion
of honeys, the prize honey of honeys, is red cedar honey. Red
as blood and as complex as an equation. It is both rare and
beautiful, and no company can fake its balanced sweetness, its
crumbling crust of nuttiness, its underlying hint of forest fire.

For no particular reason, the grounds of Nobuko's parents'
house suddenly seemed to me like some kind of private park
in which you might find a play pen with slides and a sandpit
and a little shrubbery maze which some insane British green-
keeper keeps perfectly trimmed, a hide for small animals, safe
there in those ice groups. Some ice rodent, cute like a vole and
friendly like a lab rat. I could see lights in her parents' kitchen,
early evening lights, through into what they both called "The
Den" and down into the front of the house, and low. I figured
maybe Nobuko's mother was downtown at the Ocean Trading
Company, in the herbalist district of Shokai Market, buying
some traditional restorative product. Both she and Nobuko's
father had apparently gone in for anything ancient, local and
herbal lately. "Putting their death drive into reverse," Nobuko called it, personally affronted by their enthusiasm for such
retro cuisine. Both her parents were big converts to moxa, bo-
tanic prescriptions and astringent remedies. They had taken
to snacking on Fujis of nuts and shoyu and chicory and grated
orange and took teas composed of everything from ordinary

jellyfish to aloe vera, carnation petals, silybum and cider vinegar. Both diuretics and laxatives.

"So even when they die," said Nobuko said, "they won't embarrass each other, yah, by shitting themselves."

Maybe it was better if even Nobuko's mother wasn't home, I thought, and I could wait down at the Shokai Mart myself, order a cold matcha latte or something else at one of the good Western cafés there, and maybe report the old woman's attack at the Shokai *kōban*, though I was pretty sure any witness to it would be long gone. Strange how moments of evil rely on some unknown, I thought, some empathetic passer-by to confirm them; how they otherwise disappear into speculative, fantasy darkness, inhabiting only the minds of the victims and perpetrators, just as reliably as if they had merely dreamed them.

It was then, as I reached the shiny wooden decking of the Kishimoto family home, that I saw Nobuko's mom.

I could just make her out through the kitchen window, wandering along past the breakfast bar. Naked, her neat little frame overshadowed by the hang of an American copper range hood above, wide and shining burnt umber. And the tall white pantry cupboards nearby, reflecting her in shimmering rippled ghost light. Though Nobuko's mom was in her late thirties now, her body had not let itself go much from the shape it must have always been, I suspected. A neat, sculptured like woman, I thought, painted onto her tiny bones; made for decorating with a frill of apricot linen and a blue suit cut. 1980s corporate cuts from *Tonikku* or Mont Parnesse. Nobuko's mom bare-legged on the beach at Fire Island, paddling in the whitewater, squealing like a girl, her pleated skirt out of place, out of time, pulled up around her slender brown waist. Her in their family garden in mid summer, a hot sun on her hair, shining like plastic, her cheesecloth blouse knotted roughly behind her brown wax back. Maybe, I thought, I should move away, or make a sound. Though I had seen a few women naked in our family's *ofuro*, I couldn't remember ever having felt as I did, as if something was out of place; and so I stood, staring dumbly in through the kitchen window.

"*Oya!* As if I'd just stumbled on that deer, Bambi, grazing in Nobuko's home," I admitted later to myself.

Some animated Disney version of life; Nobuko's life, in fact. And, at any moment her mom might simply slip back through the tangled green banyans and the whole moment vanish.

Nobuko's mom wandered to the fridge. Drew out a clear white wine bottle, half empty with some golden whatever, poured herself a glass and was putting the bottle back again when a guy, a silver-haired guy, a fat and furry occidental guy, came wandering out of Their Den. Who knows where he came from? But he was naked too. And he walked right up to Nobuko's mom, "that geriatric Melanie whatsit . . . *Gibson*" as Nobuko would later describe him, that "Pierce Brosnan *cho-beriba*", grasping Nobuko's mom's black hair in both his fat hands, and dragging her mouth roughly, determinedly, like some Hollywood movie-star Honcho, right to his.

3

Sukiyaki

No kidding, potentially future great cooks suffered during the Kishimoto apprenticeship. They suffered because of youth and conceit and jealousy and arrogance and rage. But one of us Chefanese died a little later that morning. Or maybe that's an exaggeration.

"So what is she going to do?" asked Keiko over the phone as I was walking toward the Kishimoto Food Company offices in Akanyio Bay and she was arriving at the creaky town wharf of Naorai, the home town of Uncle Shiro's International Culinary Institute, with Akio, Masami, Yuko and our belongings in the Company promotional van.

"I don't know," I said, "but I'm going over to the Kishimoto Food Company now and may meet her. . . . Anyhow, Keiko, what would you do, huh?"

"Gee, Koji," she said, apparently watching a sunburnt *gaijin* in a big red hat loading a cooler box into a boat about the size of one of those great new second-generation VW Beetle cars. "Fry up a bit probably. No offense, Koji! Does she think she might meet today with her father or . . . ?"

"Sure," I said, "she could do that. But would it be flip, yah, without full facts?"

"No, entirely unflip. *Choberib.* Her mother, though. There's major *giri* to consider, huh?," said Keiko, and at the same instant engaged some other gear out there in the Naorais and continued: "Or flip. What do you think?"

"I think both."

"Man it is *sooooo* creepy."

"The world is creepy, Keiko."

"*Sumimasen ga.* Ditto."

"Thank Heaven for cookery, huh?"

She realised then that the *gaijin*, who was indeed very sunburnt, looked to her as pink as the hood of My Melody in Makoto Mariwaki's *KuruKuru Shuffle* where My Melody had to stop the Spirit of Dark Power from resurrecting and destroying the world. She felt bad for thinking this.

"Only thing I know," I said, "is that she needs us more than ever right now."

"Humbly. You figure she'll make it to *Essay to Idleness* tonight?"

"She has to," I said, turning into Akanyio Bay's burgeoning media district, "the cook is her second cousin."

"That's true."

Sakana

What was it about infidelity that was impossible in Cheffanesery?

For one thing, taste was impossible to fake. In contrast, for example, sight is slow to learn and often fooled. It only recognises by practice and often forgets what it knows. Some distinguished Meiji University medical expert, who worked in a building not far from my father's, once said that this is because sight has two poles; one pole, or eye in this case, not necessarily confirming the observations of the other, but actually ritually fighting against it.

"Each eye has a popular *tatamae*," he said, "but its inner *honne* does not allow it to back down."

So all the time this battle is going on; one side of your vision challenging the perceptions of the other. All day, every day, until at night your sense of sight finally closes down and whatever great battles there have been are consigned to the darker recesses of your brain, where they re-run, episode after episode, like local television, so that even in sleep they rage on until one observation is imprinted over and above the other, leaving the defeated pole, or eye, no doubt considerably embarrassed at its loss of face.

Smell, which some older Japanese people in Spring time certainly consider their most acute sense, is slightly different. You might think that, because the human nose has two nostrils that a similar scenario to that concerning sight takes place; but this is not true. Smell is combinatory, it channels two receptors into one primary processor. In this processor confusion occurs. In fact, smell operates on a fuel of confusion, gathering and then dismissing information like a crazy laboratory of dedicated technicians trying to uncover the structure of some new and deadly strain of gastric flu. Often limited by its inability to make such pre-emptory choices, smell suffers from over-exposure, becomes tired and lazy and ultimately cannot be relied upon.

Our sense of hearing is not dissimilar. Who hasn't missed something in a conversation with close friends and then suffered the tragic consequences? Who can recognise *every* instrument played on a *Show-Ya* album, or ever wondered what the cute girl actually says at the opening of a Kei Hibiya DVD-ROM? Our sense of hearing is perfectly like that. We are each, quite literally, unwillingly selective listeners. The conduit which joins our left and right hemispheres is echoic and cluttered. Nothing makes sense here. Our sense of hearing is more fortuitous than organised.

And touch? Well, touch, all Japanese knew well enough, is by far the worst sense of all. The least able and most arrogant sense of all. Either cloying and cheap or hot-headed and cruel, touch is the sense that creates confusion, the sense that juliennes emotions, the sense that misreads intentions. Without touch, sure what could you do? But with it, how weak and how lonely do you feel? How vulnerable? Touch is a sense made for aggressors. A sense for sensationalists. A sense for clumsy waiters and salesy maitre'ds. The bright purple Toyota Crownery of senses. The fool sense. The faithless sense.

But taste? A person's sense of taste, their *jitensha*, is never faithless. Never overbearing. Never indiscrete. Never inharmonious. Never threatening. There are over 7 million taste receptors on the surface of the tongue alone, and half that again in the regions of the human mouth. And that's not the end of it. The lips can taste. And the gums. And the pharynx. And the hypoglossal nerve. And chefs, working in the realm of taste, reach out to other senses too. Cooking is both the most personal and the most gregarious of professions. It confirms our senses of sight and smell. It puts substance to our sense of sound and makes the awkward movements of our touching hands seem like the lumbering of some other creature's dinosaur limbs. It is delicate and quick and clever and keen. No wonder cooking turns out to be such an emotional art. Working with taste is like running a high-wire act over a jagged ravine for an entire American city's population. Great cooks can't hide from the responsibility of this. We can't lose concentration or everyone falls. A population runs on its stomach.

As I told Nobuko over the phone what I had seen, and she naturally cried angrily at me, I wished I could cook for her right there and then. Cook her something comforting but sharp to the taste. Like Augusto Orini cooked for Bette Davis in that damp stone cottage kitchen in that fine old film, *The Empty Canvas*. Or like her considerable staff cooked for Princess Diana, every meal that she was actually at her palace, I guess, and not detecting a mine or founding a famous children's hospital that is, as she did.

"I just don't know why she would do it," Nobuko said. "I mean, maybe she's suffering from a disease. *Hai! Cookingly!* A disease . . . Alzheimer's maybe, huh? Brain cancer?"

Though I was unsure what was involved, I said those reasons sounded plausible, nevertheless. But if there had been no previous signs then perhaps they were just speculation. "*Shitsurei*," I said, "everyone remembers: the "70s were a very very tasteless age."

"Yes," she said, and broke down again. "But why *now*?"

"Look," I said, "who knows? Parents are . . . different, huh? It's like trying to fathom, what? I guess that weird 1970s thing with that *Space Invaders* game. *Dozo!*"

Having made the difficult decision to reveal the truth, I sounded far more knowledgeable than I felt.

"I mean, what was that all about, huh? And wire Rayban glasses. That's another one. Crazy, I say. I can attend the Company meeting, if you think you need time to . . ."

"Koji,' she said. "*Hai!* You be there. I am leaving now."

"Sure," I said, listening to her draw a long, wet breath, imagining Akio, Masami, Yuko and Keiko, who I had on hold, outside the promotional van on the wharf opposite Uncle Shiro's, scuffing up tiny clouds of white dirt with their shoes.

Ohagi

Though I had not felt it seemly to openly say so, I had long suspected that Keiko was not a truly committed member of our Chefanese *uchi*. That she was, quite often, only pretending to be like Akio, Masami, Yuko, Nobuko and I. That even at school she had kept a great deal to herself and had not really joined in our long discussions of the inharmonious limitations we each found in day-to-day professional cookery. Things like: the increasing prevalence of plated hot-regeneration, where food is partially prepared and placed on plates until required and then reheated and combined with one—*just* one—freshly prepared item in order to the give the appearance that the *whole* meal has been freshly cooked. Things like: re-defining the order of serving so as to incorporate previously excess meals in new, but lesser meals. So now you can, with immunity, serve two day old halibut as sake-kasu marinated cod. *Oya!* Things like: UHT crème brûlée.

Did these things concern Keiko? I thought not. Quite the opposite. In fact, I knew personally that, in addition to the hours she had pledged to work for the Kishimoto Food Company, she was already secretly working part-time at the Ebi Ebi *sushiya* as a junior commis, and had plans to ingratiate herself into full employment there. I knew she met her boyfriend Kiseki five months ago when, although Nobuko had by then made clear recommendations regarding her Uncle Shiro's Institute, Keiko had visited the Culinary Institute of Izu-Shichito and met Kiseki standing at the ANA Help Desk at Narita. I knew Kiseki was much older and worked as a junior researcher at the Dasshimen Institute, the research college, and that his real field of expertise was *abnormal infant psychology*! A cruel individual might say that Keiko only hung out with our social group because we seemed to her the best group of persons to suit her needs.

"*Ganbatte kudasai*. You are examples of what my old world history professor used to call, euphemistically, 'an accumulation of autonomous detail'," she said, not long after joining us.

"*Ano ne*," I said, "but, what's that mean?"

"It means," she said, "that you are each gatherings of the finest pieces of a person, yah, but not complete persons contained in yourselves."

To my mind, Keiko displayed some elements of the mechanised and pedantic. Some lesser cooks can be like this, even some very famous chefs. To take an example: she never marinated anything for less than 24 hours. She would not dream of putting cranberries in a heavy based saucepan or making her snow peas "soft" or cooking a buttery mound of rice. She didn't like Kagawa's shows because Kagawa was "just like some jumped up English housewife", according to Keiko.

"*Sumimasen ga*. She's like some real first rate *gaijin* bimblo," said Keiko, uncivilly. 'No offense, Koji! Like some kind of circus freaky with one of those non-stick fryer pans. If I ever have to watch her soak a mild-cure garfish again I'll throw up. She's like a chi-chi lap-dancer trying to convince you she really, truly likes your eyes while she's also lifting your wallet. *Puke!* 'The dried wild rose petals in the picture are obviously the perfect ingredient. And for, me, too it's an *Alice in Wonderful* thing'. *O for pity's sake!*"

It was as if Keiko's cooking was always a weird accomplishment of engineering for her, like she felt she'd just built one of those ancient *hiraga* orrery representations of the known universe.

"I just like things to be right," she said.

Turns out there are a lot of persons in the cuisine industry like this.

"*Moshi-moshi!* Is that Uncle Shiro's?" Yuko asked, over Keiko's phone, describing what she saw out past the wharf.

Out across the water, through the slight, afternoon mist, a pale pink wooden turret was appearing, apparently, like the nose of a moon rocket. And then another. And, moments later, another. And then the whole of Uncle Shiro's International Culinary Institute itself came sailing out of the mist, like some sort of Portuguese galleon, she said.

"*Hai!*" I said, "I think that's it."

Iseebi-no-ikezuayu

Down in Akanyio Bay's Shokai District, the district between Shigeru, Mitumasa and bayside, nestles just about every Western food restaurant that claims to be any restaurant in Akanyio Bay. You can find there a random selection of the 20 regional cuisines of Italy, the Umbrian with its peppers and veals, the Abruzzian with its oils and pastas, the Cumean love of eggs and sugar, *Ganita all' Aranica*. A person can experience a *columbo de poulet* cooked by a real Martinquean chef. Or sit in the Ecuadoran restaurant *Cotopaxi* and order the *torta de zapallo*, which is served in a real pumpkin shell studded with walnuts. *Indian Rice* is a Canadian Place, not French Canadian, just a little Saskatoon (pinchberries and Chinook salman and the like), and *Chu Vang Nha Ga Va Nieu Tom* is nouvelle Vietnamese, one of the post-refugee places run by a guy from Hong Gai out of Hiroshima. If your tastes are more industrial, perhaps newer and less delicate, you can try *Karakorum*, the Indian place, which apparently combines the Gujarât with the cuisine of the Madhya-Mahârâshtra border, and includes a touch of southern Bihâr, from Orissa to the northern parts of the Andhra Pradesh, offers a considerable Specials menu and rarely runs a waiting list. *Huayno Huayno* is Peruvian and *Mutiny on the Bounty* is an English steak and ale joint. *Idi* is Ugandan and *Blaise Diagne* has a Sengalese flavour with a touch of the Acquaintane. It is very easy for a novice Japanese diner to feel intimidated around Shokai and there are Western fast food restaurants that have capitalised on this. *Burger King* has three outlets, *Wendy's* two, places where harassed Japanese gourmand ingénue can retreat, buy fries to go, and eat them boldly as they scurry back uptown, trying to recapture their humility.

Interesting fact: a study by psychologists at Keio's internationally lauded School of Cognitive Neuroscience showed that 10 out of 10 Japanese directly connect memory of taste more effectively with sound than with sight or touch. Renowned chefs who have capitalised on this fact include Saito Hayate, working out of *Long Road Leaving* in Takamatsu, who plays soft tubular bell music while serving an excellent Okonomiyaki-ya-European menu, and the great contemporary Italian master Arturo Risso, out of *Passione* in Boulder City, Nevada, who favours the hit songs of Frank Sinatra.

Kai

Subway carriage pulling into the station, I joined the crowd streaming up the stone stairs to the street.

Miles out to the east, over lakes and hills and parks, I imagined Akio, Masami, Yuko, Keiko and now possibly Nobuko busy unloading our suitcases into his boat, while My Melody watched them, suspiciously perhaps, bobbing up and down in his little harbour like some kind of bait. I had tried to raise them to tell them that maybe they might as well wait until low tide, but I found my big old Nokia 100 needed recharging and, because my mother had always maintained that my Great Aunt Noraline had died from ear infections brought about by using public telephones in the west end neighborhood of Boston, before it was cleaned up, I had never quite been able to bring myself to use one, and the world—Keiko, the Kishimoto Food Company promotional van, and the rest of the Chefanese—the world, for a moment, was out of reach.

Watsuki Yuko maintained that reality, the world, was it-self a taste, a sensation of calm confidence and understated originality.

"When you taste something," she believed, "you become it somehow."

I didn't know how this worked exactly, but I had seen it work. It almost always did. I had seen big individuals, *yoko-zuna* sumo-size guys, guys in giant black *mawashi* or shell-suits, for the love of Heaven, turn into what Nobuko called "cuddle bunnies" at their first encounter with white bean soup. Or ancient aunts get frisky over candied chestnuts. Food could certainly be a worldview, what my father often called in his broken, literary Japanese the *'chinchirorin'*, the chirp of the cricket that inhabits each person.

Nobuko, for her part, loved the saltiness of sea eel cooked by *unagiya* cooked at un-proposing *koryoriya* near busy subway stops. Masami loved the taste of Berebere potatoes and of par-boiled asparagus. Kieko preferred the coal-seared squab of large city Korean *yakinkuya*, and Akio chose the crusty grid-dle-blackened garfish of market *aka-chochin*. We all liked to chat with those *sobaya* cooks who occupied most of the side-streets of the Shokai District in their white coats and peaked caps boasting incredibly to me, given my *gaijin* status, about how they once personally knew Mr Boy George when he played in The Bay. How Mr George wrote "Love Will Set Us Apart" while standing at one or other of their *sobaya* and how he used to visit *Konomine-ji* temple with a boy who claimed his name was Trixie and how, if he had not left Akanyio Bay then and returned to his home in Ealing, Great Britain, we might still hear his music on the radio in Akanyio Bay right then.

Down past Sumida multi-plex and the Nankan building, with its sheer silver sides and reflecting glass, past Magna Inc. and

ATC. Nobuko, Akio, Masami, Yuko, Keiko and I sometimes reminded my younger self of Antarctic explorers setting out on a vast frozen plane of culinary disinterest. Into the outlying frosty alleyways of Shokai district with their cubby-hole Italians and storefront Korean *kimchimeries*. Passing *Furnellis* and *The Revolutionary Biscuit*, heading toward the Kishimoto Food Company's dockside offices.

Back in the 1980s, *Furnellis* and *The Biscuit* used to be great new Western spots frequented by *gaijin san* and Japanese in equal numbers. They used to be warm dark homes where Japanese chefs with backgrounds in international tourism would grill you their own version of polenta, and it tasted like sun-warmed steel. These days they're all bright and shiny and filled with graduate chefs from Izu-Shichito and Setagaya University or the Uno Tomiichi culinary scholarship and nothing they make has real punch any more. It takes *Jambalaya* now, down on Anago Lane, flaking red-paint and rusty iron prevailing, to pick up the morning mood at all and, with their praise-worthy Kenyan peaberry mochas and considerable Gautamalan Excelsos, to make a bean-to-cup statement. The scent of them leaping right over the mock arched bridge that divides Akanyio Bay from the horrible expanse of Tama.

'*"tte kimasu*," I was thinking. Out over the dockside buildings, Alcan and some of the big food company offices, Masterfoods, low-slung and expansive, CMG Providores, Golden Boy, Yonai Brothers. "Somewhere," I was thinking, "somewhere out there."

Maguro

"And that, *eeto*, was how we happened to meet up on the way to the Kishimoto Food Company that morning," said Wada Shoji, one of Nobuko's father's favourite Company Board members and now deceased, some time later, when interviewed together with us by the Naorai District police. "This young chefester and me."

Shoji had been one of the founder regional vice-presidents of the Kishimoto Food Company, when no one else in Japan was taking food marketing seriously. He was old family Honshu TV network, out of the Osaka Nightly News, setting up the media production division of the Company and, most recently, being promoted to "marketing coordination" where old food marketers with bright ideas were being put to let them graze out their time. Well into his 60s, he looked like an advertisement for Mifune Toshirô movie star surfwear or something, plumbed on his angular face and frame by a Surrealist. Back when he started in the industry, in the dark mid-1950s, everyone thought food demonstrations were just a passing phase—like variety shows featuring singing jugglers or those later, 1980s sitcoms with old middle-class American women as stars—but at that point, with recovery still a priority in the cities and, what with national feeling wanting more Japanese faces fronting imported products, and the occupying forces introducing even ordinary Japanese to new global TV networks, soon some of those Kyoto whiz-kid "cookery is not a growth industry" advertising types were looking like *koomons*. When Western supermarkets entered the picture in a big way in the early 1970s already there was excitement.

"We were like astronauts back then," said Shoji, showing his age. "Kishimoto's supermarket shows were so incredibly *next* generation."

By the mid-1970s there was talk that maybe currently famous chefs like Shohei Himeda and Sumie Mayuzumi and even a very young Kagawa might lose out to the new Kishimoto supermarket food hosts whose cooking was more cutting edge, more youthful and lively and untraditional, and who didn't expect anywhere near the fees or expect those added "luxuries" that a big *aji* like Himeda, for example, who apparently required an entire UN fleet of colorful motor scooters even to get out of bed, expected.

Yes, cookery was suddenly big grassroots business and the Kishimoto brothers were very encouraged by their first year's figures to launch into more media-driven campaigns. All that parental stuff about a meal being a place of quiet contemplation, and therefore the wireless radio certainly not being left on, and about not eating dinner while you watched TV, quickly went out the window. With food marketing you could eat while your meal was being discussed; you could choose your last dishes while consuming your first. Or, if you are venturing into Western cuisine, howabout asking an "expert" if your *rinones al jerez* should really be tasting like onions? All this suited the Japanese way of life.

Wada Shoji was one of the pioneers of this TV food marketing and, although rejected by big advertising companies for many of those first few months, and openly ridiculed by traditional Japanese marketers, who viewed all the new interest in cookery as either an attempt by the occupying forces to feminise, and therefore, weaken the population, or simply as a passing phase, he didn't seem to have lost face in their earliest snubs. We had a feeling though that, in the small thin acreage that was Wada Shoji, some rich field of concern might be growing.

"Whatcha, *maa?*" he called, getting out of his cab.

It was typical of Shoji to take a cab. The guy could buy half of Akanyio Bay but he liked to travel public, striking up conversations with anyone about the future of electronic billboard-advertising and Mr Tom Cruise's love-life and the size of the budget at the Onta Food Trading Company and the role of violence in hugely successful film franchises like Hosokowa's *Kinkyū-no* series and just about anything directed by Takeshi Kitano.

"You all for this meeting?" he called to me, leaping up onto the pavement.

"Respectfully—not my gig, Shoji-san," I said, talking to Shoji as he would talk to us. "I am trying to pay humble respects to Mr Kishimoto for his considerable sponsorship and support but can't seem to find him."

"Right, right," said Shoji, getting closer. "Hey, but you know, he won't be in the office for almost a full hour yet."

Futo-maki

Interesting fact: Manuel Cabral Amaro, recently voted one of the most outstanding chefs in the world by *Culinaire* magazine, noted for his highly inventive and exciting Macanese cooking, particularly his balaya (spicy Goan rice dish with seafood or goat meat), and his crawfish *goona* (indigenous seafood and vegetable stew), was the youngest of 14 children, and began cooking for broadcast purposes in his hometown at the age of just 6. Cooking brings families together; it can also, equally, tear them apart.

"I simply love these Xicanos," roared Shoji, leading me into a corner booth in *Julio's Kitchen*—pleasant little Akanyio-Mexican place off Saiko Square. "*Shitsurei!* In a Western economy in which 53% of the population work in the service industry you get standards. It takes true character to have respect when taking out another man's garbage."

In *Julio's* the oregano hangs as thick as louvers through the air. On the wall, behind the till, there is a big portrait Shoji told us was of President Ernesto Pone de Leon who was apparently going to lead Mexico out of its 20th Century poverty

with innovative irrigation schemes and highly competitive re-
location deals for North American manufacturing companies
who chose to relocate to places like Querétaro or Villaher-
mosa. But the companies didn't come.

"The problem," Shoji said, "as every Japanese would recog-
nize, was skilled labor."

They could, maybe, import their own from those popu-
lous and highly competitive cities of the Los Angeles hinter-
land or from the blooming biz-tech regions of the American
East Coast but the cost would be enormous and the social
consequences—displaced Simpsons families, golf-partner
angst, fueled nouvelle drug habits—difficult to predict. They
could, maybe, train the local population, the Xicanos themselves, but the danger there, humbly, was that once they were
trained they too would disregard Mexico and leave town for
some fabled forested northern city where they might rise up
the ranks of Anglo society like warm winds through a dank
old house.

"Manufacturing is an uninventive and workaday industry,"
Shoji told us, formally. "A Mexican President, whose popularity rating was high, but whose national product was low
should have chosen cookery instead. People will travel for
food, *ayu*. They will seek out cuisine's origins and then bask
like sunfish in them."

I had already read that a lot of well-known Western cooks
have founded restaurants that capitalized exactly on Shoji-
san's principles: Irena Palanuik's *Arté*, which served a notable
arrosta porchetto and nestled in the high peaks of the Adiron-
dack Mountains like an American bald eagle atop a cliff; Lao
Tsu's mighty *Mei Kuei Lu*, which hides safely in a small back
alley of Qingdao, as if threatening to pickpocket its patrons,
and apparently couldn't be faulted on its *chiao-tzu*.

"Food," Shoji had long been telling us, "is undoubtedly a magnet. Some big *ikas*—Yuharu Ryu for example—claim to have been dragged around the world by it.

"*Maa*," he could cry at that point, "enough already!"

"The way I see it," said Shoji, folding this long coat sleeves around his thin arms, "I grow more concerned about what will happen today by the moment."

"*Sumimasen ga.* How's that?" I asked, fearing that Shoji-san might think me too forward for asking. But unable to stop myself. For some reason I was thinking that Nobuko's parents' garden might well support the growing of coffee beans. Some Jamaican Blue Mountain. Some Tibetan Green. Who knows, maybe some Guatemalan A1. And her mother could dance naked there in the coffee fields with her occidental lover, like some kind of aging Tokyo striptease act.

"Well, *mago,*" continued Shoji, cupping his own Kenyan in his small hands like he was a field mouse, "you may not know this entirely, but there's a feeling at the Kishimoto Food Company that the future of food marketing lies elsewhere. Not with campaigns such as the *ashita no masutāshefu* apprenticeship program and not with TV food programming.'

I tried to speak but couldn't quite form anything audible before Shoji went on.

"*Hai!* I know. I know." He shriveled down into the bench seat, disappearing into his giant suit. "I have tried to show them that the figures are great. I have tried to explain that apprenticeship programs such as this tap into some the primal contributions of young persons and we would be ill advised to ignore the possibilities of that. I have humbly outlined Yushio-san's position thoroughly. But, *mago*, they like bright packaging with sports persons endorsements more now. You know, "Hideo Nomo says 'I eat Dotonbori Fish Cakes. They make me run very fast', 'Kano Jigoro says 'There is Nuthin' more

Refreshin' than Kirin Beer', "'f the ball is very difficult, I take Caramint Sweeties' says Rancy Valentine of the Chiba Lotte Marines Baseball Team.' They've been involved in such *nemawasi* discussions for some months. What can I say?"

"*What?*" I might have said, had I been older. But I just stared dumbly.

"*Hai!* I know. I know. Respectfully, who am I to make any impact? I think what they really want to be is insurance salespersons, frankly. Cookery shows . . . *ayu*, they think they're just too old fashioned now. They say their clients no longer want to sponsor them. They're even talking about having endorsements from pop pop music acts on their very own albums instead. Aaa! Like Bub Geldof, yah? Webbed Aids or some *chikooshu*. . . Whatever it is. I think if this very big promotion of Yushio-san's doesn't grab them they just might . . . "

"Oya!"

'*Hai!* I couldn't agree more," he said, and pulled his lapels up to cover his narrow chest, as if in the spicy heat of *Julio's* he was cold. "Well, that's my news. *Aaa!* Anyhow, how are things looking for you these days, *majo*, at your Kishimoto Shiro's cookery school?"

Cooks imprint themselves on you with the same jurisdiction as their food. In nearby *Jug-Jug*, the walls mocked up with made up grass and the food predominantly calabash and pigeon peas, Takeshi Mike, the Head Chef, claimed to be a Caribbean born *gaijin*. He was not Caribbean. He was born in Yokohama City. I knew for a fact that he had never even been to the Caribbean. But there wasn't a Caribbean place in Akanyio Bay at the time he opened and Mike, whose mother was from Fukui and father from Yokohama, had an idea. Tatsuya Wada and Kazuo Sugai of the Moorish-themed *Moro*, in Aomori, were not Moroccan. Did this matter? That was the kind of thing Jacobo Tatti had tried to teach me in my two weeks with him.

"A cook is what?" he said. "A trinket. That's what. Be what you have to be. Your patrons must leave your place wanting to take you home."

Was Tatti actually Italian? No. It turned out he was born in Birmingham, England, and only travelled to Genoa to found his restaurant and cooking school. Did he really once own those London restaurants called *St. Martin* in The Savoy, *Vico* on Bleeker Street, and the *Award-Winning No.11*, where reservations are taken only for regular customers? No, but he worked in these places and many others and he knew how to talk about them as if they were his old apartments, places he grew up in, where family still lived. Other than that, he was an old creep. A Grecian bouffed occidental scam merchant whose credentials were false, who preyed on young hopeful cooks, who thought it was convincing to say that baked clams were de rigueur and once told my mother that Motoki Uyeno's Venetian cooking at the *Venus Restaurant* in Nagoya was very good. That was why I returned to Akanyio Bay to finish school in order to go to Uncle Shiro's Institute. Did my parents know that? In Japanese terms, they would have lost considerable face had they found out.

Interesting fact: suicide among cooks is three times higher than that among office workers, despite urban myths concerning insurance clerks with automatic weapons and commodities traders who entertain, and then eat, their colleagues. Cooks suffer far more, overshadowed only by the suicidal tendencies of teachers, emergency medical personnel and police-officers.

Shoji, silent and small, seemed to be listening to the sounds of *Julio's*, the maybe-Mexican chefs out back preparing their *frijoles refritas* and their fresh *botillos*. Shokai up the stapes, the morning traffic humming along bayside, delivery vans bringing mineral waters and restaurant linens and servicing Electronic Point of Sale systems. Then Shoji let fly.

"You are the ones now, *mago*. The ones."

The waiter who had served us drifted over to suavely slide out our cups; while Shoji seemed to be marking time, licking his lips as if they were food themselves.

"I'm dying, *ayu*," he said, finally. "*Oi* big drama here. *Sumimasen ga*, get the cameras up close on this. *Aaa!*"

He caught himself up, his small sharp nose poking vertically toward something we could not see in the far right corner.

"*Aaa!* I could write the copy for this one myself. Your *sofu* gets the word that he hasn't got long. What does he do? He calls his kids and tells them he's going to resign from his employment. '*Aaa* enough of working!' he says. His kids don't know why. It is out of character. They get defensive. They grew up with dad working at the Kishimoto Food Company. They've never known anything else. And their father doesn't want to tell them. He loves them impossibly, huh? He wants to wind up his big selling season like he always would. But then he thinks: what if it all just *yoboyobo*, huh? What if the last thing he ever does is some red lantern *chikooshu* promotion or a Kodomo-no-hi Special for the HWT Chûgoku Public Broadcasting Network. What if that was all he had?"

"What could I say?" I said to Nobuko and Akio, Masami, Yuko and Keiko later. "He was sobbing by that stage. Sobbing his big heart out. Shoji. Figure that. *Oya!. Our* Shoji!"

"I remember when Yoshio-san and Shoki-san went their separate ways," he said, out of context, dreamily staring out into the street. "*Aaa!*" And then back to his situation:

"You know what the statistics are for heart disease in this country, *ayu*?" he said. "Well, if you don't mind, I'll tell you: there are 22.5 million obese people in Honshu alone. 22 million. *Aaa!* And you know what causes that? . . . *Food!*"

"Those sad, fat *nasus*," he said. "*What do they eat?* What for the love of *Heaven* do they eat?"

"With all this going on, why two brothers would separate themselves from each for so long over some thing I'll never know," he said. "The Kishimoto name is respected every-where. Shoki didn't just found a cookery school, he forgave his brother many things. And he him."

Suddenly Shoji was laughing so hard his jacket was jumping all over his tiny frame.

"Mutally," he said, getting himself back under control. "Mutally, at least, they forgave. Anyway, now the Kishimoto brothers are talking again *Aaa!*, and Wada Shoji is dying. Who knows why? Some weird *chikushoo*. They don't even know what the Heaven it is. They stuck a camera up my *koomon!* Can you imagine that? Me on the frontside of a TV screen. My ass at least. Ha! *Hijō ni Amerika!*"

I told him, bold as I was now, that that was probably what it was like to be really famous: having your *koomon* on screen. I had no idea what else to say or how else to respond.

"*Aaa!* Yes," cried Shoji-san. "Finally. Wada Shoji's *koomon*. You think whatshisname? – your Jerry Brockhammer—could cope with that one, ayu? You think my ass might go a full pro-gramme season on your ABC?"

And then the great Shoji just fell back in his chair, with his shoulders cranked over and his arms kind of hanging down by his side and he looked into that red light of the restaurant, like everybody does, *Julio's* is just so redly lit, and he said, in this creepy but kind of touching old voice:

"So that's it, *ayu*. What is it you call yourselves? . . .The Chefanese? That's it. If I am humbly able, I want to make this apprenticeship program Yoshio-san has planned the greatest cooking promotion that has ever been seen in Japan."

4

Kaki dote-nabe

"The greatest show Wada Shoji has ever produced. *Aaa!*", Wada Shoji told me. The best cooking apprenticeship program we'd ever see. It is not difficult to imagine this now as a dream sequence. Like that portion of the very popular movie *Moon Struck* where the actor Nicolas Cage sees his future in Sonny and Cher's shimmering reflection in one of her mama's green blancmange. Or the bit in *Deep Content* where Johnny Deep confronts a perfectly lifelike robotic version of himself without being concerned about the spiritual consequences of doing this. Creepy! Uncle Shiro's apprenticeship program was going to form the basis for the most incredible TV cooking promotion anyone had ever seen in Japan, that's what Shoji said to me.

"Battle of the Little Bighorn," I joked. "Custer!"

"*Aaa!* Those guys! Custard's last stand!" Shoji replied. "Do they think Mr Wada Shoji hasn't produced great TV before this?"

In fact, he most certainly had. A whole raft of 20th Century Japanese TV cooking classics.

"Groundbreaking promotions!" he went on.

Like CR-TV's *Wild Foods*, about foods that for long time have been ignored by persons but that might sustain you if you were trapped in the mountains around *Bandi-Ashi*, for example, or out in *Daisetsu-zan*. The KOC-TV Special about the world's greatest cheese products. And who knows how many episodes of *Fitness for Living*?!

Of course, Uncle Shiro's junior high graduate apprenticeship program was not, strictly speaking, television at all: its purpose was to introduce his young students to the regime of hard work he expected at the Institute and to create the sense of team spirit that would endure during his classes. Nevertheless, it was ideal for what Nobuko's father and Wada Shoji had planned.

Shoji said the show would, in truth, be one hundred times more admirable than anything Keije Hidari had ever done. Many times better than Yuharu Ryu's shows or Chishu Ozu's

"Better, *yah,* than Kagawa's," Shoji said, looking at us as if we were something he'd just now stumbled on in the glittering chamber of Tōshōdai-ji and its burial mound or something. Something he was encountering on a surprise trip forward to another Japan in another time.

"And here is why,'" he said, laughing out loud, "because Kishimoto Yoshio's show will be *entirely* . . . Chefanese!" But I thought he just appeared so honest and sad.

"I'd never seen anyone sounding so immodest," I told the others later. Sometimes Nobuko still cries when we remember this.

Natto

Out in the Naorais our Chefanese registration at Uncle Shiro's International Culinary Institute should have been well under way, Akio and Masami and Keiko and Yuko working like cogs in new and mighty gastronomic wheel, turning slowly toward ignition.

But dreams sometimes take time to unfold.

Interesting fact: the most common complaints about res-

taurant menus are A: that descriptions of food are vague and unhelpful; B: that the pricing is unclear; C: that a language which is not the customer's own is used to describe the choices. In Japan, according to the Government Trade Act of 1973, it is an offence to falsely describe goods or services or to supply any good or service to which a false description applies. 4 out of 5 queries in Western restaurants in Japan relate to menu descriptions.

"O, just look at this place" said Keiko, standing in the balcony door of one of Uncle Shiro's student accommodation to which we had all been assigned, looking out into the fog, and talking to us on her Nokia.

Keiko frequently reminded me of the character called Velma in *The New Adventures of Scoobie Doo*. All those sightings of unusual or inexplicable phenomenon and possible criminal types. Keiko no doubt got a lot of that from Kiseki, with his unusual interests in psychology.

Frankly, Nobuko had no intention of sharing that room with Keiko, but because she had not arrived yet, as I thought she had, and because Yuko and Masami and Akio were still over on the mainland unloading the Company van, Keiko was stuck registering all our names at the Institute desk, to save confusion, while somewhere out there, "Somewhere," I was thinking, back over in Akanyio Bay, other trainee chefs were travelling likewise toward all of us.

"*Moshi-muoshi*. It looks like a handprint by Umehara Ryūzaburō here," Keiko said, still staring out, I guess, across the foggy water.

"Huh?" I said.

"Two green mountains," she said, her phone going in and out of range. "A red afternoon sun. And a seagull."

"Sure thing, huh?" I said, not imagining any of this, imagining the room, instead, was like something right out of that well-known 1990s TV series *Seven Brothers* in which an ancient Hachinobe family is caught in a perpetual battle with marriage and maternity. Ito Masatake, whose recent death by *seppuku*, then starring.

Out in Uncle Shiro's quaint old foyer the first of the other trainee chefs were already milling. Already around a dozen of them. Young trainees who Uncle Shiro had apparently found on his private trips to the West Coast. On trips to the North and South. On quiet nights when he left his International Culinary Institute and did not return until some days later. On weekends when his staff assumed for some years that he was respectfully visiting the graves of he and his brother's parents. But no. His leather kaban later slung in the corner with luggage tags and flasks of clean drinking water and him sleeping it off. Some he found on longer trips he made unannounced to places well beyond Hokkaidō and Honshu, which he didn't often reveal.

"Rumour has it," Nobuko told us later, "that my uncle smells the food of potentially great cooks. And then somehow he sets out and tracks them down."

Out on the road in search of not food, but actual chefs. Cooks who were ready and willing to pit themselves against other cooks. Like boxers, only with food. Cooks who Uncle Shiro offered that big chance to confirm once and for all if they were good or bad.

"If you really, *truly* want to know, that is," Teini Eiko, Uncle Shiro's assistant, wrote to each of us in his letter offering us places.

Trainee chefs, whose food he tasted, who he observed, and then who he selected for his International Culinary Institute, so long as they competed in his apprenticeship program, a

competitive training he organised each year with the determination and care of a Japanese Olympic Team Captain.

Two weeks previously he had apparently flown to Sasebo
and now here were four crazy-looking trainee cooks from a
school in Sasebo's Chinatown standing in the first year student kitchen:

"What is it with Hokkaidō guys?" one of them was saying
in the direction of Keiko, checking in. "They never know how
to use pork."

All this is recorded for posterity on the Institute's old fashioned CCTV.

"*Konnichiwa.* And, what, they don't think a mallard duck
is food?" he goes on, possibly drunk. "How many types of
mushroom they know, huh? Ever heard of sea spice? What
about cuttlefish?"

No one takes up this call; but the foyer looks as lively as a
Kodomo-no-hi parade and the trainee chefs that are there are
surely not people I recognise, though some might already be
on their way to fame. None of them plated hot-regeneration
chefs. None chefs who would rather order in pre-sliced bulk
portions of Western foods than trim them and slice them
and portion them for themselves. None overly enamoured of
high-capacity microwaves, bake-off products, electric knife-
sharpening stations, frozen vegetables, catering mixes, burger
presses, bespoke counters or automated peelers. They were
artists. These were the potentially great chefs whom Uncle
Shiro had chosen.

Rumour was, Nobuko heard when she arrived, that some
of Uncle Shiro's chosen young trainees had, secretly, already
begun to plot together to ensure they did well in their competitive traineeship.

There was no evidence at the time to say this was true.

The Kishimoto Food Company's offices were quiet when I walked in. Silence too, Yuko once told us, was one of the undeclared negative results of the constantly shifting modern culinary experience.

"These days everyone expects a great restaurant to be totally, utterly silent," she said. "*Oishi desune?* Unless they're family restaurants. But what family restaurant is great, and who ever actually *eats* in a family restaurant anyway, huh? A family restaurant promotes noise in order to mask the terrors of day-to-day domestic living. Alternatively, any restaurant where Western haute cuisine is served is all caught up in this silence thing, so that the pursuit of the genuinely contemporary prandial experience goes serenely undisturbed by the sheer uninventiveness of their food. Largely, that's it. There are occasional bizarre ethnic variations on this situation now all over Japan, of course."

The Brasserie, for example, was one. It was breezy and sometimes had live music. The Bistro, alternatively, was most often more darkly lit and promoted blackboard menus. The Lounge & Grill or Bar & Grill emphasized its drinks menu, which might include international beer specials as well as house speciality wines. The Café was casual, though sometimes ironic twists will be made on this fact. The *Rink Water Café* in Nagano was one example of this. There tangy chevres and creamy blue cheeses met stately halibut in porcino foam in an atmosphere of dire, portentous seriousness. The Eatery, the Tavern or Taverna, the Roast, the Inn and the Diner offered mostly subtle interpretations of all these basic locational themes.

"Culinary volcanoes," Akio said when we were each sitting in the Otori Department store, hosting our sponsor's food products. "I hear that's what your uncle is seeking for his International Culinary Institute."

"*Hai!* So, if we are successful, we might just erupt, huh!" said Nobuko, waving a flag for the Golden Valley Tea Company.

"With respect," said Akio, standing up in the large sea eel costume she was wearing. "I mean young Japanese cooks who are not at all set in their ways and also as solid as rock."

"Hey, what about then," said Masami, looking sheepish among his colorful collection of Tanuki glistening fruit filled jelly, "we do something to cement this great friendship of ours, yah?"

"You mean, like getting a *irezumi* or something?" said Keiko, shaving cups full of colored Hokkaidō Ice Supply ice. "All those needles, yah? Just for some kind of a warlord picture or something?"

"*Sumimasen ga*," said Masami, "something else.'

Two nights later, after we had finished work, we went down into the old trading quarter of Akanyio Bay, to a small dark shop down near the furniture market that didn't look likely to ask our ages – "It looks like something out of King whatsit's. . . *Tutencumin's* tomb," Nobuko said as we walked in.——and we had ourselves branded.

On my right eyebrow shone a small steel stud.

"Mine reminds me of one of those little silver bandees they put on pigeons, huh?" Akio said, who'd chosen to have her stud in her belly button, fingering her raised flesh as we all walked out of that little trinket shop.

"*Hai!* Just think of it as our Chefanese radar," said Yuko, her stud sticking up from her eyebrow.

"That a fact?" I said. "What—if one of us loses his stud then all of us lose him, then?"

"*Ganbarimasho*. First thing first, though," said Keiko, who said her pierced right ear was stinging terribly. "A cook must be true to her kitchen."

Mizu-yokan

The Company's cream colored boardroom was cold and clean.

Mrs Akatsuka, who managed the Company's reception team but perhaps, some thirty-years ago, back in her teens, should have joined the Coca-Cola Company in Sapporo she never stopped talking about, stoic and smiling-faced, but often displeased, was over at the Gaggia making a latte for someone, who might have been Bibby Nijo, a young *buchoh* we all knew from the Tanuki Sweets Corporation, but at that point I couldn't be sure.

Interesting fact: the average Japanese family-run restaurant has an advertising budget not exceeding 1% of its gross annual turnover, we were told in our training. This compares unfavorably with the advertising budget of almost any small independent grocery store, which averages out at around 5% of GAT, and the advertising budget of the international kitchen products firm, Boneedo, which comes in at 8.5% GAT. Is it any wonder some *nomiya* and *ryotei* in Japan rely almost entirely on repeat business?

During day-to-day business the Kishimoto Food Company's offices were crazy: senior product representatives everywhere, planning out new strategies, teams locked in long discussions about forthcoming promotional events, new product trials in rooms here and there, with persons paid to humbly offer their reactions, all around the Company offices creative teams mixing and meeting and sometimes even only conflicting.

"Food McHell," Masami called it, when her first saw it, but since then we had each come to enjoy our visits to the office, our meetings with our sponsors representatives, our discussions with product planners, our assisting with new product tastings, which we then hosted for real in supermarkets and hotels and malls.

The fact is, it was not always easy at the Kishimoto Food Company to reconcile the ideals of the boom period Japan with the evolving ideals of the new more austere age. Some of the older staff members, the *senpai*, made reference to the Company's important creative heritages and notable firsts, even going as far as to suggest their strategies were a direct line of inheritance from *kabuki*. They'd say entirely immodest things like:

"We've been putting food on Japanese *kotatsu* for longer than I dare to think" and:

"Who eats only to live! Our campaigns say: 'eat also for excitement'."

To counter these arguments *kohai* members of the team, who were mostly Hokkaidō-born or of half Hokkaidō-Honshū parents, and had recently chosen careers at the Kishimoto Food Company over other possible lives as website designers and graphic artists, key encoders, *tanshin-funin* automobile executives, commodity traders and so forth, would match this immodesty with sayings of their own, like:

"Nobody wants those crazy old campaigns any more, yah."

And: "The thing about food is that it should not feel it is your entire life."

And: "Don't you think hosting is so incredibly 1960s now anyway?"

And: "We're simply meeting the demand of the new consumer. What are you doing?"

There seemed no easy solution to this growing conflict.

The voice behind me caught me off guard.

"The Cucumber Man," it said.

Standing there, Nobuko's mother looked unsettled. Understandably, perhaps.

"What?" she said, closing the door to one of the many Company meeting rooms behind us. "Shrimp Man? Ice Maiden? Japanese French man? Aren't all these things you are, Nitta Koji?"

We all liked to dress up to cook, not only when hosting, but also to make a point about the subtle changes of taste and enjoyment that are produced by appearance.

"Cooking is a contact sport," Yuko once said to me, word-choosing, "and people have to come to understand that."

I watched Nobuko's mom patrol the room's perimeter, looking out high up there over Akanyio Bay so that when she finally spoke it seemed to me that her words came from outside, rising up somehow from the pavement:

"Mr Hinds usually works at Ford, but he has a secondment," she said.

"Did I . . . ?" I began, but then held my tongue, when bizarrely I realised Mrs Kishimoto was addressing not anyone else but me.

"He is currently a visiting Professor of Computational Systems at UBC."

"You make secondment sound like a terminal medical condition," my 14 year old self thought.

I have often wondered since: was I in love with Kishimoto Nobuko even at that moment?

I think every one of us Chefanese had been in love with Nobuko at some point. Beauty, everyone knew, was more than skin deep: it was as deep as possibility and as broad as persistence. Nobuko liberated our Chefanese souls; even mine, though I was so much not like the others. She was like a resistance fighter or a clearer picture. I think the day I met Nobuko in the café of Shimura Junior High, and realised she was the daughter of Mr Kishimoto Yoshio, was the day on which I finally understood what it was about cooking that drew me even then. She said I should stop reading and come with her and meet some of her new friends, who turned out to be Kuroda Akio, Watasuki Yuko, Yonai Keiko and Saionji Masami.

Keiko said: "There's two important things you can do with your life, do you know them?"

"Cookery," Nobuko replied, "that's the future for Japan. My father's company has evidence that over 80% of modern Japanese families list food as their primary source of joy. Does Mr Shibatani tell you that in his history class, huh? When is it that any of Mr Kindaichi's literature classes matches those expectations?"

"If there was a great chef cooking in every Japanese home every night,' said Masami, "and you could be there with them, imagine the things you would experience, *yah.*"

We all agreed that we had an equal desire to put choice in everyone's culinary vocabulary. That the food people ate was an indication of the choices they had in life and that most Japanese we knew had no choice at all.

Yuko said: "Frankly, *yah*, if a person can't imagine anything more interesting than a mochi what does this say about their view of the world?"

"So imagine this," said Nobuko, "a good cook is totally indispensable. How many people, anywhere, can say that?"

Nobuko's mom circled me.

Interesting fact: although the Mississippi Delta is world famous for its food as well as its Blues music very few Americans have actually tasted any of its cuisine. While Spiny Lobster, once considered "poor man's food" has made its way onto the plates of first rate dining rooms, stewed chitlins, collard greens and fried catfish are largely a mystery to most Americans who listed them in the category of 'Would Not Eat' when recently surveyed.

"Nobuko's father is leaving me," Nobuko's mom said.

Alarmingly, I laughed out loud, breathy and too quick like a whisper from some kind of amphetamine amplified Ginza dancer.

"That's not true," I thought, in the background again.

Do we ever really think as teenagers that our parents have love lives and that, if they do, they could possibly be complicated? Is it possible our parents' resent this and therefore make space in their lousy schedules to conduct sexual experiments that far exceed the boundaries they themselves would ordinarily have set? In this way, you might ask, do Japanese children actually encourage the acts that create themselves. Perhaps this is what the great writer Kawabata Yasunari meant by "the sublime power of self-creation."

"Respectfully," I said, unnerved, "I'm not sure I . . . ."

"But you came to our home," said her mom, "and Mr Hinds is an old old friend. Surely you want to know this, *ah*? Nobuko's father was leaving me before he and I ever . . ."

"No!" I blurted out, for no reason, other than my embarrassment added: "American?"

"Australian," said Nobuko's mom. "Jasper and I met when we were at art college and . . ."

Gross slippage, I called this: that in my foreignness I had not been able to tell the difference between an *Amerikan jin* guy and one from *Ōsutoraria*. I sometimes got the feeling that my yin as it was called, which was dark, moist, receptive, earthy, female, and my adopted Japanese side, and my yang, which was bright, dry, active, heavenly, male, and my American-born side, were preparing to fight to the death.

"Why then?" I thought, in the background. "Why would he leave you, huh?"

Nobuko's mom seemed unable to go on. In fact, it seemed to me to be impossible for her to say very much more at all to anyone, she just went all porcelain and prim and I couldn't quite dislodge the idea that I'd broken an irredeemable law in seeing her as I did, some law of nature and she was being generous by not rising up and clawing me to death. Then the door swung open and Nobuko's father strode in. Wearing a red shell print shirt and a tan like a monkey. Silver haired, toothy and anvil jawed as a pterodactyl, he reminded me quite a lot of that 1980s American TV star, George Hamilton, only Japanese. And her father was not alone either.

He strode in with Shoji-san, and they were laughing and barking out what I realised later was an old, obsolete Akanyio Bay Buffaloes team chant which went something along the lines of 'Itsu! Itsu! Itsu!', or something, and Shoji had his right arm around Nobuko's father's shoulders and her father had his briefcase and a bunch of flowers from the florist concession downstairs and, as they came in, with a team of *senpai* product managers behind them, and department managers of a number of key client companies and two steno-pool girls looking just like *shingeki* Marilyn Monroes in How to Marry a Millionaire Nobuko had a vision which she passed on to me an hour later, driving in the Company van to see her second cousin cook at *Essay on Idleness*:

"My father, Koji," she cried. "Has discovered he's gay, huh? Isn't that flip?"

"*Sumimasen ga*," I said. "How do you know?"

"*Hai!* I just worked it out," she said. "That's why my mother could not talk to me and talked to you instead."

"Oh."

"Who'd have guessed, huh?"

Embarrassed, I asked again how it was that she knew this, but she seemed to be watching the road and just said that surely, finally, me of all people got this. I said maybe she should talk to him. Get his story and so forth:

"What do you think?"

"But, Koji, I'm sure you see," she said, swinging into the carpark at the restaurant, "this is so *soooo* supreme! No more rich little Akanyio Bay girl, huh? Finally I can stand up and be counted as human."

Chawan-mushi

I waited in the foyer near the board room for Mr Kishimoto, practising what it was I would say to him, my considerable apologies for disturbing his time, the great obligation I felt to him, my deepest *arigato* and apologies for the inconvenience my living was causing him. But when Mr Kishimoto emerged he did not stop. Rather, he marched very very quickly right past me, his face alarmingly like the face of a ghost, his head thrown back, his arms hung surprisingly limp and hardly regal by his side.

It was not until some days later that we discovered what was decided at the Kishimoto Food Company that day:

The retiring President's promotional idea, they had said, was a great idea, in fact, and all the sponsorship companies in the room had indeed arrived to offer their humblest support it.

The great man no doubt, they said, respectfully, was also much aware of the change in the nature of Japanese eating. Who better, after all, than the man who had jointly founded such a company as this to recognise those changes?

Respectfully, they said, such things as interactive sports shows, for example, popular music shows, WAP, high savings rates and limited consumer purchasing power.

Yes, they were sure, their retiring President knew exactly about all these things. They awaited, in fact, his discussion concerning them.

What a fine thing it would be for the Kishimoto Food Company to promote the food products of its clients through his brother's young person's apprenticeship program, with a show produced by the honourable Mr Wada Shoji. What an honor, and as Mr Kishimoto Shori, his younger brother, lately declared as the company's majority shareholder, had voiced his humble willingness to take over the Presidency the appropriateness of such a campaign could not be more plain.

It was clear that Nobuko's father had no idea that was coming. None of the usual *nemawasi* discussions had heralded it for him. The impossible had happened. He simply had no idea.

The room apparently fell silent. Nobuko's father rose a little, his face red and white in succession, muttered two words which Shoji did not catch, bore himself stiff and erect for a moment against the table edge, and then sank down in his seat like a very large stone.

5

Usuyaki tamago

Interesting fact: While preparing a dish of squab with cabbage, Madeira and Spanish onions, Marceline Valmore, chef de rottisseur at the then little known *La Poule* restaurant in Saint-Malo, France, in the summer of 1904 was surprised to see her onions turning bright crimson in her oval cocotte. Repeatedly, in fact, she found the onions took on this crimson coloring, without the aid of herb or spice and, to be frank about it, it was doing very little for the subtle complexion of her squab. She experimented further, tried Bermuda Onions, they say, and even leeks, though her inclination was to favour Vidalias on account of the Bermudas being far too sweet, and therefore causing her cabbage to sweat. Regardless, both the Bermudas and the leeks took on the same crimson hue. I guess they looked like something out of that horror movie, *Wes Craven's New Nightmare*. They were, as it turned out, drawing the iron oxide through the enamel of her cocotte and reacting with it. She changed pans to the only other instrument she had clean, a copper salmon kettle, and the coloration ceased. By alternating between the salmon kettle and the cocotte she found she could turn the crimson coloring on and off at her will. Even better, she was able to bring out a subtle radish-like flavour, a complementary flavour to her Madeira and a brilliant accompaniment to the light texture and subtle tone of fresh squab. Thus *Onions Pcule*, a significant historical moment in the evolution of the *soubise*, or onion sauce, and one of those interesting moments in the story of the spread of great cookery.

Nobuko, as unaware as I was of what had happened at the Company, rang the reception bell at Uncle Shiro's International Culinary Institute for what was the third time, while Yuko, Masami and Akio stood behind her with their cooking equipment and those expensive cameras their parents had given them as going away presents, and My Melody, My Melody the *gaijin* boatman, stood behind them at the Institute's main entrance, looking exactly like that kind of occidental man-mountain we had all seen in a million Walt Disney *Cartoon Nation* programmes, the Bluto man, the Yoshimite Samuel, that huge red hat of his clasped in his hands and his shiny pink head glistening in the late afternoon sun.

"Looking for Mr Kishimoto?" he said, in English.

"Ha! How do think, mister?" said Yuko, in Japanese, smiling too sweetly at him. "We would just walk in and ask to see Mr Kishimoto, huh? What, we look like farm-persons?"

"*Sumimasen ga*. Decidely not," he returned, in smooth, unaccented Japanese, "I mean to say: right place, yah. But, with humblest apologies, the Institute Director greets all his new *gakusei* personally."

Yuko shrunk back quietly, Nobuko's ringing of the brass bell covering her embarrassment, at least a little.

There was no sign of Keiko. We all figured she was with those older trainees who were already inspecting Uncle Shiro's institutional kitchens, which Nobuko said were perfect: large and shiny in the way of outward looking Japanese kitchens of the immediate post-war period, those 1950s Japanese kitchens all full up with utensils and homey magazines featuring new-wave film stars such as Shoichi Ozama and Masaomi

Kondo, *Good Homemaker* and *Restaurateur*, everything polished and laminated and cleverly folding away. Big could certainly be beautiful. Ovens like saunas, enormous tilting boiling pans, a micro-wave free-zone, whole banks of deep fat fryers frying merrily away. Nobuko said we would all check in now, and while we waited for Shoji to arrive we would go out to *Essay on Idleness* and see her talented second cousin cook, and then maybe meet our class mates, discuss with them maybe their sauce rouilles, their elderflower vinegars and their marinated turbot. Nobuko seemed to have put her mother's occidental lover out of her mind, at least for now; and, flying with the idea that her father might end up a *New Gay* magazine icon. "Like Sulvester Stallone or Dolphin Lungrin or someone, only Japanese," she said, was punching holes in our anxious suggestion that we might not do well after all in the apprenticeship program.

"What, surely you were there when the best American cuisine the great Shinsusaki Kawazu could come with on her TV show was a 'Reuben Sandwich'?" she said. "Pah!"

I couldn't say, after the morning I'd had trying to pay my respects to Mr Kishimoto, that I wasn't pleased to be back among my fellow *rakugo* and to join a little in Nobuko's momentary boastfulness.

"Les Salon Chefanese," Yuko was bolding calling us as we walked around the Institute's gardens, watching the other new trainees arrive.

We couldn't help but value the thing that had drawn us all together in the first place. All of us turning up late for classes on "Promoting Economics" and "Dealing with Sports" and discussing quietly in the back row how, if any of us ever had the gumption and good sense to one day leave Shimura and pursue our own cooking careers, it would be unlike anything anyone had ever seen.

"We could even do the Paris Toque d'Or," said Masami. "Ah! All those second rate junior commis pruning around talking about who does a better red pepper coulis or who has a better take on gnocchetti."

"Or the *Salon de Cusinaire*,' said Yuko "That sucker, man, it's like a dog show!"

"Or the World Master of Culinary Arts," I said.

"*Sumimasen ga*," said Nobuko, "how about nothing where cooks have to nominate their earliest food memory, huh? Or name their favourite after-work meal? Or show how they use their favourite kitchen tool, a slotted fish spatula, a mandoline, and so forth? Or outline in three words how they relax?"

"Certainly," said Yuko.

We wanted to make our careers a genuine homage to what we would learn, and build upon, at Uncle Shiro's International Culinary Institute. Cooking that knew no boundaries. Cooking with the same passion as people devote to eating.

"Isn't it true," Nobuko said, formally, "no person likes to imagine the meal they're about to eat is the result of a less honest imagination than they think they have displayed in ordering it?"

"*Kore wa nan desuka?* Man," whispered Masami, a touch too loudly I guess, as Uncle Shiro's Registrar appeared at the Registration Desk, "was this *ika* once in *Metal Licker*, you think, huh?"

Coming out of the security room behind the desk Tieni Eiko sure did look like someone out of rock and roll's Heavy Metal period, his mahogany colored hair long and tied back in a greasy tail, his suit kind of too large, deep blue and velveteen. He made me think of one of the thoroughly aged members of those classic American bands: *Bon Jovi* and *Lone Bizniz*.

"Honourable apprentices?" he said, punching something into one of computers on the desk. "*Onamae wa.* Names, heh?"

Yuko leaned long-armed onto the front desk next to Masami. 'Watasuki Yuko.'

"Ouch," said the Registrar, typing this in: Watasuki. "From Shimura, heh?"

Then he stopped what he was doing and looked us all over.

"What is it with Shimura this year, heh? Cookery explosion? Ha! Get it? Cookery explosion? *Bing! Bang!*' He madly typed some more. "There are six from Shimura. One arrived already. That right?"

Reaching down onto the desk he read something and grinned strangely at us and said:

"And a note from Mr Kishimoto asking that you are to be housed in the East Wing." He click-clacked through some more information, muttering:

"The East Wing, heh? Six from Shimura. And an *Amerikan* too! What in Heaven . . . Shimura school. *Sheesh!* Make cooks in Shimura, do they now? Ha! *Kushakusha!* Not to my knowledge. What the . . ."

"*Shitsurei.* Don't mind me," he said, much louder, as if suddenly realising we could hear his muttering. "Always crazy-pa this time of year. East Wing,' he said sliding keys to each of us across his desk. "Classes commence at 8.00 am in the main hall. Mr Kishimoto says to you . . ."

He read out from a card fixed to his desk.

"I welcome each of you to Kishimoto's International Culinary Institute. Be considerate. Respect the needs of others. Discover all you can here. Remember the brave are often the least foolhardy, but also the most adventurous. *Ganbatte kudasai!* Cook wonderfully. Our teachers welcome you. Our staff welcome you. Your consideration is appreciated." He silently read something else on his PC screen to himself and then looked us over for what seemed like a long time. "Film stars, heh?" he said finally. "*Bing! Bang!* Mr Kishimoto says he hum-

bly welcomes you and wishes his brother's campaign show a
great success.'"

"Humbly," asked Yuko. 'When does the show happen?'

"*Dozo! Dozo!*" he said, quite suddenly, and loudly, pointing
us toward the reception room. "In good time, yah. In good
time. *Ja mata!*"

"How strange," whispered Nobuko.

Niku

Out at *Essay on Idleness* the restaurant parking lot was filling
up with diners. Keiko still wasn't with us and the general feeling in the minivan was that if she didn't turn up very soon
we should tell her that if she wasn't going to be a part of our
group anymore then maybe she should tell us so. Or, at least,
that was what I was saying.

"Respectfully," I said. "None of us here are foolish, and not to
turn up at a time like this is . . . *oya!*" I pointed at the stud in
my eyebrow and each, I noticed, reached also for their own
Chefanese studs.

"You don't like her, Koji," said Masami, finally, stepping
out of the Kishimoto Food Company van.

"Unfair, huh!" I said. "*So desuka?* Who says I don't?"

"You don't," added Nobuko.

"I have some feelings, yah, that no one is entirely indispensable," I said, boldly.

It was my youthful inclination that Keiko's absence had
something to do with her crazy older boyfriend, Kiseki, and I
could just imagine all these poor, gum-shoe wearing, Game-
boy playing, inner-city kids falling down on beige colored calf
leather lounges beside Kiseki in some Psychology Institute ex-
periment where they're served up several different types of

mushroom and asked to define "Which one is a Matsutake?" Or placed in a locked, pastel colored room, no doors or windows or anything, with a giant bowl of almond custard, their hands tied behind their backs, and only one chopstick to use and told to "Show us how you eat this without spilling any."

Essay on Idleness, on Route 974 at Ukiyoe, was an authentic Japanese-American Blues brassiere. It offered what food educated people had been saying was the best Beef in Juniper Sauce in Hokkaidō, inspired entirely by the long and prestigious history of the renowned *Coca-Cola* company—the famous founder years with Mssrs Pembersan and Robinton, Mr Chandlo registering that now worldwide trademark, those brilliant slogans "The Pause that Refreshed" and "It's Really the Thing" composed by that genius of Food Marketing, Robert Woodruff, and so on.

Her second cousin, Tohru Hira, Nobuko had heard, who had convinced his father, when Hira was barely a teenager, to change their little backwater *nomiya* into a faux Big Rig Chicago-style truckers stop meets *Coke* themed American brassiere, was as crazy as a cupcake, rode a Harley Davidson motorcycle to work in his apron and clogs and had more cheap tattoos than an *bōryokudan* gang member.

I figured all this was part of his carefully cultivated image. Hira had just graduated from Nemura Senior High himself and been accepted into Uncle Shiro's Institute on a full senior traineeship, which his father had naturally announced in large banners above their brassiere. Japanese cooking, after all, is nothing if not an egotistical art. You can't simply prepare a meal, you must prepare a meal to elicit a reaction. Internationally-orientated cooks in Japan go through all their lives seeking out swooning and surprise. We combine garlic with almonds, explaining that we are simply making an *ajo blanco*, but really we are determining if the Japanese diner can detect one Western taste in the other. We never leave poultry alone; but, instead, might stuff it, for example, with egg whites and shallots and morels and pine nuts and, by doing this, create a ballotine. We braise in beer, sauté jellyfish, smoke rainbow trout, macerate fresh fruit, sweat spring onions—being artistic in temperament, but grounded in absolute, unshiftable gastronomic practicality.

What senior trainees had Uncle Shiro, who had apparently that day assumed the company Presidency of the Kishimoto Food Company in preference to his older brother, chosen for his Institute?

Had he chosen with uncompromising precision? Made surprise visits to tiny senior high school classes in remote Japanese coastal towns? Had he gone to city restaurants with real big reputations and long-reservation lists and watched new, talented dishwashers fighting it out to become sous chefs? Or maybe to Western-style cafés. Even to cafés. *The Café Blu. The Café Paradiso.* To those increasingly popular Northern gastro-cafés, where young persons straight out of Akita College or just back from a year studying in California, were making precocious gastronomic statements, much against the tradition that the greatest Japanese food is obtuse and complicated and only served properly by *chefs du cuisine.*

And did he not stop at that? Visiting street vendors in Fukuoka and schools down in the Hanshin Industrial Zone. Fried catfish and chitlins joints in Chiba, that barbecued kangaroo place at Kansai International Airport, where Osaka Senior High School leavers dressed in bizarro bottle green t-shirts and white cowboy hats and something they referred to as "thongs", kept wanting him to try their "Australian bush foods."

All this, so that when the first of his senior trainees arrived in the Naorais he had already constructed what he thought of as the ideal pre-requisites for his apprenticeship program, junior cooks who could not simply *match* each other in their desire for traditional culinary skills, but go way way beyond this, who wanted to mix their cuisines, work from scratch, make it up as they went along. Was Uncle Shiro, in fact, intending to make a statement about the future of Japanese cooking?

"I was honored, humbly, to be accepted into our Uncle's Institute," said Tohru Hira, lifting red peppers from a sautè pan with a perforated spoon.

"*Hai!*" said Nobuko. "As are we all."

We watched in awe as he cooked some espresso beef for a pulled pork tamale, wrapped a heart-shape of home-cured beef with baby leeks in caul fat to keep the whole firm and tight and attractive, turned out two saddles of hare on a base of forcemeat for a couple who had travelled all the way from the Tôhoku district just to eat there.

"Best. New. Chef," Nobuko whispered to me, a look of alarm on her face. "Sheesh!"

Masami, unable to control his enthusiasm, watched openly.

Hira, suddenly noticing him, was almost certainly embarrassed.

"I hear, respectfully," he said, trying to ignore Masami as we tried not to watch him shimmy over a bratt pan to carefully stir what smelled like a Zinfandel-Chilli Sauce, "that Uncle Yoshio is producing a food campaign to accompany the apprenticeship program?"

'*Hai!* That's true,' said Nobuko.

Out in his father's restaurant what looked like a mix of truckers and salarymen and travelling gastronomes were eating such dishes as Bresaola Singing with Sherry Vinegar and Mushrooms Duxelles. Whizz-hipped Tohru sisters were wheeling around the place sliding plates onto tables, looking like a whole family of Japanese Marilyn Mansons.

"I'm sure your skill will be rewarded," said Nobuko finally.

"*Oseji dake.* That's just your flattery," he said.

"If this is the standard of the competition," Akio whispered to me, "what chance have we got?"

"*Hai!*" I said, "but perhaps . . ."

Masami photographed Nobuko's cousin with us, Nobuko and I either side of him and the him, his tattoos kind of like pop art subway graffiti when you looked closely enough, all down his arms, a collection of dragons and snakes and statements about sharks and making war against Yamaha riders.

Interesting fact: many famous cities around the world are named after food. Chicago, Illinois, for example. Its name is derived from the native American word *Checagou*, meaning "wild onion."

We photographed our soon-to-be fellow but more senior student, Hira, in his father's kitchen, Nobuko talking to him about their shared family, his love of great butchery, a well-boned roebuck, pork blade-bone, skinned hare, prepared grouse, croise duck, Crown of Lamb, in light, naturally, of the increasing vegetarianism of modern consumers and the popular movement against animal products.

Masami photographed him with Yuko and Akio laughing nervously as they rode with him on his Harley in his parking lot, looking like Japanese Steve McQuones, they said, as the dark dusk sky opened up and the rain set in, lashing across the carpark in great movie-like swathes. We said, sure we had seen the winner of any culinary competition even before one started, and we made our way back.

"*Shitsurei shimasu!*" Masami called from the van window as we drove off. "We'll see you at Uncle Shiro's."

"Yah, Masi," said Yuko in the front seat, "you think maybe you might put back in your tongue now? You never seen a person work with red meat before, or what?"

"Now I know why my father wanted me to meet him," said Nobuko.

"*Sumimasen ga.* How so, Nobuko?" I said.

"Don't you see, Koji. He wants me to try some other occupation. Tohru Hira is suppose to discourage me from cookery."

"*Shitsurei!*" said Yuko. "Let him try."

Odori

Unable to sleep, haunted by the idea we would disgrace ourselves, even before we have celebrated our fifteenth birthdays, I saw the sun rise on Uncle Shiro's International Culinary Institute at exactly 5.18 am, shredding the last remnants of a moist grey fog that hung low on the dark water. 5.18, that was closing time for some Japanese chefs, opening time for the world.

The others still sleeping, I was out on Uncle Shiro's lawn watching the Naorai District fishing fleet and lobster boats tearing up the dark blue channel between the wharf and what I guessed were the Naorai shellfish grounds. Rumbling and putting around the brightly colored lobster trap floats, they looked like crazy mall shoppers, back and forth along the red and yellow float lines, lifting traps, emptying them, dropping them back into the water.

There were other local folks awake too. Tieni Eiko, the rock-n-roll Registrar, out in Uncle Shiro's stroll garden, feeding a local cormorant a slice of something. A guy delivering oysters, lumbering back and forth over the stone bridge which connected the island to the mainland now that the tide was low. Someone, unseen, down in the boat harbour, banging away metallically in the engine bay of some ailing old trawler.

Down in the town, where everything was still closed of course, I found a Tru-Value Dime store with all kinds of amazing historically illuminating bargains like "Kappa-maki, Five for the Price of Three", "Cassette Tapes" and "Kerosene." A bank, an antique store, a gift "emporium", a dentist, a Toyota dealership with only three cars, an Estate Agency going by the name of Eiko & Son, which I figured reflected the college Registrar's respected place in the District, an abandoned dairy the size of an aircraft hangar, some rundown waterfront *ryokans*, which looked remarkably like love hotels—each with its *dai-suki* theme, one with turrets and battlements, like a European castle, another like a pyramid, a third in flaking silver, calling itself *Hotel Science Fiction*, each with their own optimistic "Vacancies" sign—a garage and marine supply store, two seafood shops, a chandlery, a ladies "Fashion Store" and seamstress service, a bait and tackle shop, a hardware barn, a *yakitori-ya*, until I had left the town itself and was down on the old dairy wharf, stretching down from the abandoned building and along to the waterfront. I could see something bobbing down below on the beach now, on the low tide line. Bobbing, and slowing rolling back and forth as the wash of the boats out in the channel came lulling on it. But it was not a simple thing to get down there and I don't know what drove me on, maybe that the others were still sleeping and maybe, because of that, that I had no reason to be awake in Uncle Shiro's Institute, before our first class, and before I knew if I personally would ever be a great international cook. Maybe, had they been awake, I wouldn't have gone. Had the others been awake and we had been able to plan out the day, our first day, then things would have been different, positive, filled with opportunity.

Instead, I was over the rail and sliding down the embankment, onto the beach, where the sand was cold and coarse and hardly yellow at all. A dog, barking now somewhere back behind me, in the town I guess, made me think of cheap eatries, horror bars with *yazuka* bosses and *soba-ya* for industrial estates, and the engines of the boats on the water sounded way way too loud. I thought I could see My Melody in his dinghy over near the harbour, his red hat blinking in the rising sunlight, but now I was focussing on something else, the water lapping against my shoes.

And Keiko, who it was, was humbly lapping back, bumping the shore with her head, her naked back washed over with that blue water, her legs splayed and tillering back and forth, and her arms, "Reaching out in front," I told everyone later, "just like she was a mermaid diving down to the bottom of the sea."

UNCLE SHIRO'S INTERNATIONAL CULINARY INSTITUTE

6

Uji Gori

"No doubt about it," said Yuko, "as this terrible thing proves, making love to cookery is like making love to a ghost or, *eeto*, maybe a memory huh? One minute your lover is right there beside you, and the next minute. . . . As Shoji would say, *seishin shûyô*:

"'A planet revolves humbly 'round the sun. Yet which is more dependent?'"

"But Yuko," said Nobuko, "with apologies, where does one single person really meet another anyway, ever, these days? *Kuso!* Entirely and equally, not just physically, *ane*? If they did, maybe this thing . . ."

"I really believe some of us Japanese people have been badly affected by what Mr. Oshiro says is the passing of the 20th Century Japanese ideal," said Masami, word-choosing, as we watched the black and white Naorai District *keikan* van in the street below our room, with the Naorai police milling in increasing numbers now around it.

Mr. Oshiro was the Modern Japanese History teacher at Shimura Junior High.

"No offense, Koji! Traditional things like *shochu-mimai, ka-raoke, On* and *majan,* for example," continued Masami. "But, also, low interests rates and high centralised public spending, my father says."

"Frankly, *oi*," I said, "every one of us knows that with a good thing potentially always can come a bad one. No offense taken."

I thought of the old *gaijin* cleaner woman who had attacked me on my way to pay my respects to Nobuko's father and wondered if any of the others had detected anything in my report that the bruises on my arms and swollen cheek were the result of "falling, surprisingly, out of bed."

"I mean,' I said, "Meiji scientists as well as philosophers have written about such universal challenges, right?"

"So we six meet in the good and evil world of what, gastron-omee?" asked Nobuko dreamily, watching the police interviewing the Kishimoto Food Company salespersons unloading food products from the company vans below. "Cookingly! Is that right, Koji?"

Nobuko and Akio and Masami and Yuko and Keiko and I at Uncle Shiro's Culinary Institute like Chefanese Lords in the tremendous Chefanese universe of Chefanesery. That was the plan. Each of us new royalty in the mighty apprenticeship program. Like outrageously unrivalled, unmatched, and unmatchable, cooks working side by side in a kitchen so brilliant, so amazing, so creative, that other Japanese cooks would press their hot red noses to our tiny latticed windows to watch us work, drool over how we orchestrate our youthful team, wonder how the Heaven anyone gets here from where they are. The tastes. The smells. The adulation.

Could we really become the world's first Chefanese superstars? Sponsored by the Golden Valley Tea Company, Big Boy Seafoods, Tanuki Sweets Corporation, Hokkaidō Ice Supply and the Taifū Beer Company? Life in the domestic Japanese hospitality industry does not often have the potential to be that incredible. A commonly heard complaint in the *kowareta* steaming short order kitchens of the Nibonbashi District is:

"Work hard, *otootosan*, and achieve almost nothing."

But we each had much bigger plans and, as we watched the police milling below, it was far too easy to imagine bigger plans sliding away. Plans to work on cruise ships maybe, for example, when we were older. Cruise ships where, though employment conditions are often tough, the pay is good and the world is your oyster. It is possible, in these jobs, to find gastronomic employment on several oceans in succession. Popular cruise lines servicing the Hokkaidō ports of Sapporo and Nakodate include: P&O Cruises, Radisson Seven Seas, Pacific Cruise Line and Cunard and Seabourn. Modern cruise ships leaving these ports have a low guest:staff ratio, encouraging individual attention and personal service. Earnings are largely tax free and, while the accommodation may be somewhat minimalist, the tips are superb. All those drunken, vomitory ever-so-grateful old diners.

Likewise there was work, perhaps, with ski companies, like Herman Scott Ski or Voyager Holidays, for example, to quote from a well-known brochure around our high school. In these job directions companies provided not only the requisite free accommodation and meals but also heavily discounted travel opportunities. Young chefs here could ski all day and work at night. Though, it's worth remembering, we told our sensible young selves, that these positions were decidedly seasonal. Other alternatives, particularly favoured by the energetic Yuko and the pragmatic Masami, included: resort work, with exotic locations as exciting as the Maldives, the Caribbean and the Seychelles. And, favoured by the contemplative Akio, work in Safari Parks in Africa where drivers and trackers led novice safari tourists into remote locations. Though heat and humidity could be an issue, a free vehicle and private healthcare were said to be most often provided.

But wait a moment! *Wait a moment!* I must rewind. . . .

Down on the beach, I pulled Keiko from the water, clasping her half by her shoulders and arm and half holding her up as she seemed to belch back into life, both us by then crying for help.

"No!" she gasped, strangely. "No!"

"Keiko!" I cried.

She barely looked at me.

"Keiko! What is this?"

I began to make out, from her spluttering, that this condition of hers had not been her doing.

"How did you . . . ?" I continued.

"O *sumimasen,* Koji," she spluttered, unthinkingly. *'Keisatsu o yonde kudasai! Just look at me!"*

I turned away, abruptly realising that she was naked.

She was barely able to breathe, coughing at that the same time that she would always be obliged to me, always be grateful for my kindness in saving her, *osewani narimashita,* the greatest of debts to be me, the most intense obligation, the completest and most humble thanks and so forth, retching up intermittently, in great shuddering belches, what seemed like whole oceans of grey colored sea water.

Keiko shivering and crying in a heap, I quickly gathered her clothes which were strewn, strangely, in the shallow water on the island's edge, floating like a mad artist's rendition of a Japanese girl — *"Chotto! Yoisho!"*—the *maiko* dancer in the sea. Her crying more so, but with more intention, more clearly, saying something about someone having hit her from behind, pushed her.

She re-dressed herself, sobbing, her deep red t-shirt and blue jeans clinging to her, and dripping. I tried not to look.

Leaving her plumped on the wet sand, I could think of nothing else but to quickly make my way back, toward Uncle Shiro's.

Taku-an

There is a popular saying among many older Japanese inhab-
itants of Hokkaidō that "From Catastrophe comes Life. *Somo
eiga niwa orijinaru no saundo-torakku ga tsuite imasu ka.*" The origins of this saying have a great deal to do, quite naturally, with
Mount Asahi, Hokkaidō's steam-venting volcanic peak rising
above the entire island as it does, snow-white and flat-topped
like a space saucer. It is said that all life on Hokkaidō once
emerged from Asahi-dake, alpine flowers blooming there, up
from its base, like snow flakes returning inch-by-inch to the
sky, and bears and pika in its towering pine forests, scarred
by lightning and poisonous ash. *Tama* and *tamashii,* the divine
kami. To be damaged, but not to die, my father said, is a dec-
laration of your innate lack of Enlightenment, your human
failing in sinking into arrogant comfortableness, and your acceptance of punishment for this.

"You, *musuko*," he said, "reap your daydreams. All this
cookery, huh, what kind of future is it?"

"Poor Keiko," whispered Akio breathlessly, as we stood at the
window watching *keikan* vans arriving across on the mainland,
and the police gathering on the front lawn of Uncle Shiro's International Culinary Institute.

"But what was she . . . ?" Nobuko began, hardly awake,
trying to focus.

I went bumbling into the details: the sun on the clear green
water, and Keiko all but drowning there, stripped naked for
Heaven's sake, and the dog barking in the background, and
My Melody-Jiggery clanging away over in quaint little Naorai-
Go harbor, beyond the rundown *dai-suki* hotels, and my heart:

". . . fast pounding, *kuso*, like I was running up a mountain,
huh, or something?"

"Crazy, crazy . . . ," Yuko shouted. "*Chikushoo!* What is it with her, going out by herself like that."

The whole of the tiny waterside town, opposite, already seemed overrun with police and, downstairs among the other new trainee chefs, someone was saying that already reporters were arriving.

"Keiko is . . ," Masami asked, "alright you think?"

"*Hai!* I think so," I spluttered. "I only was able to bring her back."

"Koji-san, the great detective," said Yuko, smiling to herself. "Dick Tracy, huh? Magnum PI? You run on back, then you called security, huh?"

"*Hai!*"

"At least she was not . . ." began Nobuko, trailing off.

We each finished her sentence for her, silently.

"I wonder now, yah, if her family will let her stay?" said Akio, looking out the window at the police tramping back and forth across now watery rock bridge.

When Mr Tieni Eiko emerged from his office to speak to the press he looked more like a Heavy Metal rock star than ever before, with his dark wide sunglasses pulled back tight on his eyes and his mahogany hair now loosely falling on his shoulders in permed and intricate ringlets reminiscent of coarse loose wool; and, expressing his sympathy and regrets to the respectable family of Yonai Keiko, said that, for reasons of respect and also legality, Mr Kishimoto's Institute must, for now, offer no further comment.

"Your uncle is a smart man, Nobuko," said Yuko, maturely, watching Mr Tieni fielding the reporters in the Institute's Western-style dining room. "With a circus like this best, yah, to keep out of the way."

"*Hai!*"

For a moment, Nobuko studied the reporters scribbling on their pads.

"Only, I wonder, incidentally, where is he, though?"

I couldn't help thinking the same thing myself.

Hadaka-maki

That morning both Shoji's mom and Nobuko's mom arrived. Within minutes of one another, though in separate vehicles. Given Mrs Kishimoto's new life, and Shoji's determination to make the most of his dying, I wondered if their timing was not entirely fortuitous. But neither seemed aware of the irony of the moment and greeted each other on the steps of the Culinary Institute with a torrent of arms and tears that reflected their long friendship. Shoji had worked with Nobuko's father for years and most of the Kishimoto Food Company's more spectacular food campaigns owed their origins to this association.

A light rain had come in under the fog and was falling slowly, strangely warm, and darkening the sea of the Naorai District into something like lead. There in the Convention Room, we milled with the other young apprentices and more senior trainee chefs, Hiro holding court on the best way to fry a loin of venison, and Akio all but sprinting away at the thought of trying to cook an aspic d'oeufs de caille au caviar, or even an Eggs Benedict, in such prestigious company. Awaiting the arrival of police who had asked to take our statements, it seemed that rain was swirling right up to Culinary Institute, joining the fog that had already ground away at its upper stones, leaving it low and vulnerable in the water. Now the rain took the rest and, to add strangeness of things, when, finally, later that morning, the fog lifted and the rain stopped the sea had risen up so far that the bridge had entirely disappeared.

Interesting fact: frozen foods have become increasingly popular in Japan these past few years, even with the very best cooks in the very best *ryotei*, because of the fact that, even after several months in a deep freeze, and regardless, incidentally, of the presence or absence of sophisticated and expensive packaging, or *oya!*, that is "freezer bags", few vitamins are actually lost. The general public, however, is yet to be entirely convinced.

We were each released into the charge of Mr Tieni.

"Rest, *Bing! Bang!*" he cried, as what seemed like the entire Faculty now emerged from the kitchens to stand behind him on the stage in the Convention Room. Each in a tall too white toque. All in pure white coats, pockets embroidered with "Kishimoto's International Culinary Institute." Distinguished from one another only, with respect, by the designs of their baggies, which were not as I'd suspected they would be a universal sea of black and white checks, but in all colors and patterns, some particular and serious, deep greens and plum colors, some bright and lively, yellows and reds and purples, and some in crowded, mad patterns, prints of kitchen utensils and types of vegetables and varieties of peppers and the word "cuisine" in Japanese and in English.

"All this bad business," Mr Tieni barked suddenly, tipping forward on the narrow wooden heels of his pointed brown boots. "*Shitsurei!* Makes for bad cookery."

"Go!" he cried.

"Go!" joined in the faculty. "Rest!" Rest, that is, before the rigours of the induction commenced late that afternoon.

Our sponsors were due in after lunch and Shoji, ever the professional, wanted each of us Kishimoto Food Company hosts to be photographed with them. Them and their products—Golden Valley Tea, Big Boy Seafood, Tanuki Sweets, Hokkaidō Ice Supply, Taifū Beer—them and their display stands, all bright with electronic displays and the smell of their products, and us cooking and pouring and passing things out on silver trays.

Meanwhile, Mrs Kishimoto, preoccupied it seemed with her new lover, "the great Mita Mikko is trying to recapture her youth, huh?", as Nobuko was calling it, had disappeared in a boat in the direction of the small islands of the Naorai and, for the moment, we were left on our own.

Successful young cooks in Japan, maybe who are twenty years old or the like, have a look about them, an attitude, a *punpun*. They stand loosely in their Western clothes around cafes and *kappo* and *nomiyas*. Make jokes about the blandness of modern Korean cooking, the madness of Indonesian, the way Tibetan handmade *tse bhale* leaks with cabbage water. Chew gum. They're bold and brash and, compared to the rest of the population, not inclined much toward modesty. Tradition strikes them as a strength, but still they fight it like spies, sliding away into the Western restaurants that sit awkwardly in the food districts of Japanese cities like speckled hens in a pen of pullets, in order to try Halloween Cupcakes and Pea Souffle, and experimenting with mace and celery seeds and juniper in their cooking, regardless of their acerbic strangeness, regularly, but secretly, reading *American Gourmet* magazine. They travel for work. They travel for pleasure. They're like hawks or dolphins, migrating to remote places to bask and mate. Their conversation is rapid and restless and full of possibility and speculation. They talk about restaurants they've visited and what they found there:

"Man, in Kuala Lumpur, can you believe it, they stuff chickens with Brazil nuts? *Shimatta!*"

"No kidding, yah, and in West Africa, minced meat is mixed with almonds. *Yerk!*"

"But that is nothing, you know, compared to the appearance of street stands in Lima. Nothing whatsoever. Think about those animals mixing with eateries and the like. Greasy everything. Vegetables with no colors. *Oya!* Even several types of cheese pie!"

and

"Man, you want to talk animal fats? Try *Cowboys Hall of Famous*, New York City."

Interesting fact: the London Institute of Caterers and Hoteliers in Great Britain regularly runs classes for visiting *rakugo*. The subjects available include such topics as "Exploring Hospitality and the Catering Industry", "Recognizing Customers" and "Methods of Providing a Food and Drink Service", but also "Reading Modern Literature", "Transcendental Philosophy" and "World History." According to their attractive brochure, all these courses are regularly oversubscribed.

We made our way out from the island, in one of the Institute's little red punts with Harding, who we had known until that moment simply as the My Melody Boatman, plumped at the tiller in his big red hat, and with Hiro, who had kind of attached himself now to our Chefanese group. He had done so largely because he was Nobuko's cousin, but maybe also, I thought later, because he himself was afraid. Afraid that what had happened to Keiko had some connection with us, with our forthcoming studies. Afraid that, in the end, he might not be as great a cook as people thought he was. Afraid that his style might be too brash or too adorned or too forced. Afraid that diners would not appreciate what he had cooked them. Though Akio was still in awe, and Yuko really didn't seem to like him, I thought of him more as a privileged aesthete, a culinary monk, than as a student competitor, hidden away in his father's brassiere, cooking his sauces and his pan fries, drinking strong American coffees, contemplating both his successes and his failures. I wondered if he had ever seen ordinary food hosts at work, or watched some of the short order cooks in the Akanyio Bay aka-chochin securing eel to their chopping boards or skinning cuttlefish or sliding a muki-mono knife through the coarse outer leaves of a cabbage. Had he experienced real cookery?

"Too mighty Power Ranger, yah, for me," said Yuko. "*Oya!* And all those tattoos? Like visiting an art gallery every time you see the guy. Or, what, a local Kyoto *yakuza* gang end of year party?"

Rumour was that the apprenticeship program was to be overseen by a panel of three Master Chefs and that, if Kyoto Kagawa wasn't maybe going to one of them, which was not so far denied, then certainly Yitsuko Sasaki was.

Yitsuko Sasaki who, as a young chef himself, had cooked in *ryotei* all over Hokkaidō before leaving for Europe. Who had endured those years in the later 1960s when having a Japanese cook in your Euro-restaurant was like having a fine bamboo plant or a sitar player in your foyer.

"Kensington-Orientals," Noboku's mother called them, or sometimes: "Orimentals! Ornaments mostly, yah."

How many cooks had left Japan in those years to cook purely Japanese food in the West? Only to become after a while a passing trend. Restaurants with names like *Shubashiri* and *Toki-no-Kane* in the Midtown East District of New York or in Soho, London, or in Frankfurt, becoming by the 1980s *The Shuba Place*, *Big Noodles* and *Toki Jim's* and selling also fish-n-chips and 'Eastern dips"!

Yitsuko, who had thereafter established himself as one of the leading exponents of *sappari cuisine*, giving perfectly defined taste to the otherwise exorcised liveliness of banning marination and reducing menu choice, that was the aim of those *sappari* chefs.

What an honor, everyone was thinking, to be selected as the International Culinary Institute's most impressive apprentice by a cook as esteemed as Yitsuko Sasaki. Likewise, no doubt, the other panellists would be of equal stature. You could not possibly fail to distinguish yourself after being chosen as best apprentice at the Kishimoto International Culinary Institute by master chefs like that.

As we travelled across the water, the rock bridge sloshed and spat in the sea right beside us. The high tide falling now, it looked like a prehistoric creature that awaited some suitable ship so that it could rise up completely and, growling like a tornado, swipe it aside with its huge and scaly claw.

Harding, who seemed to me to be one of those occidentals who'd come to Japan in search of meaning and found, instead, complete mystery, whistled constantly as he punted. Some popular tune that I couldn't place, just softly and distractedly, watching us, until finally he spoke, firstly in Japanese:

"What's your speciality, huh, *oitokosan?*"

I looked beneath his hat for some indication of what he meant, but for the moment nothing emerged, just the steady hum of his tune and the equally unfamiliar hum of the punt engine, his mouth easily mistaken for the engine box.

"Food, *takenoko*," he said. "What is your *speciality*? Vegetarian? Chickens? *Makunouchi bento?*"

"O."

What he was saying suddenly clicked into place. . . .

But as I went to answer, I found I could not.

At first I was drawn to say "Seafoods", the sea chopping at the punt, as it was, and the Naorai turning a dark olive green in the afternoon sun. Growing up in Akanyio Bay, container ships vying for places beside fishing vessels and ferries and flat-bottom punts, there was no doubt that *buri* and *ebi* and *ika* and *maguro* seemed like accessible ingredients. But if it was seafood that I saw as my future, then what about the rest, the cuisines based on technique, barbecued, broiled and so on, the national cuisines, the madly hot Mexican, the simple Chinese, the careful French, the German, the Argentinean, the Kosher, the panoramic American with all its foie-gras foams and roasted beets and Arctic char and Pacific snapper and buffalo and loin of spring rabbit and . . .

"I have no speciality," I said, finally, almost gathering the words back in as they came out.

"No speciality!" he laughed.

"No sir," I said, "I don't . . .', and wished I hadn't spoken.

"None?" he cried.

"I . . . "

"You don't cook *age-mono* and *tempura*? Not *mushi-mono* and *tamago-yaki*? Not *yakimono* or even *teppan-yaki*? *Aya!* You're not a curry man? You don't make *ham*burgers? No? . . . No hamburgers?"

"No," I said.

He cut the punt at an angle across some steely sea chop and then settled it down to its steady forward hum again. "You don't cook spaghetti and other pasta dishes? Chickpea fritters, maybe? Squid?"

"Respectfully . . ." I began.

"Respectfully," he barked back. "Not lobster *fueillete* or duck *rilletes*—served with cornichons, maybe, and pickled onions? Not sweet pork sauce or chicken empanadas? Not kale and *linguiça* soup or *barbounia*?"

As he was speaking he seemed to grow more red, taking on the hue of his hat.

"Not thin slices of *viande des Grisons*, so nicely air-dried, served with a small bowl of spaetzle noodles and dumplings and veal medallions in a mushroom sauce. You don't do that?"

He cut the punt motor back a little as the rocks of the tiny Naorai-Go harbour appeared.

"*Nan te iu ka?* Sea scallops in a Parmesan-cream sauce. Garlic shrimp sautéed with *pepperoncini*. Octopus, shaved and marinated in mango. Grilled tuna and eggplant-fig tapanade. Baby lamb with buckwheat sprouts and red peppers. Warm goat's cheese sprinkled with honey and raisins and served on a bed of polenta. You don't . . ?"

Reddening further, he seemed also to be changing in shape, growing somehow, perhaps with the trick of the light as the old houses of Naorai-Go appeared through the light afternoon fog, and the punt rocked from the wash of the harbour and a fishing boat, passing, sounded its bell at him.

"Black-pepper Snapper. Linguine with baby clams. *Pollo al horno*. Swordfish steak. Shrimp Spring rolls. Barbecued quail. Scallops with lentil and coriander sauce. . . ."

By the time we were pulling up to the wharf, Akio, Nobuko, Yuko and Masami talking now about how they might greet their sponsors this afternoon, Harding seemed to me to have grown very large indeed, his face now glowing red and his arms, as he tied the punt to the wooden steps of the wharf, all hairy and silver, and his torso quivering with its rolls of stuffed flesh and its fall altering as her shifted it from one side to the other, holding himself steady against the wash.

"No food speciality," he said, turning the switch on the punt engine to make it stop, "but a *rakugo*'s food speciality is . . ."—the engine idle now, a lapping silence had fallen, the others above, clambering up onto the wharf – "a *rakugo*'s food speciality is . . ."—he licked his lips and his tongue seemed to be the size and color of a brown bear's—'eeto, well, shimatta!, it's *his voice!*"

"Guy sure does like his food, yah," said Masami as we walked away from the punt, Harding loping around on the steps.

"Be careful he doesn't eat you alive, Koji!" cried Yuko, clacking ahead along the wooden wharf. "A real cowboy as big as that."

"*Hai*," I replied quietly, thinking about what Harding had said, "but he just might be right maybe, yah."

Tsumire

As we came to the end of the wharf a familiar figure appeared ahead in the street. It was Keiko. She was in the arms of her boyfriend, Kiseki, and emerging from one of the rundown waterfront *ryokans*, the flaking silver one, calling itself *Hotel Science Fiction*.

When she saw us landing at the wharf her boyfriend, Kiseki, waved. So bright and so breezy.

"She's alright," he was calling, his face strangely the color and maybe also the consistency of a ripe Golden One peach.

"Absolutely fine," he called again, guiding her down the little street by the crook of her arm.

I wondered if he meant anything specifically psychological by this, something he'd picked up around the Dasshimen Institute, where he worked, something about the aftermath of attacks of this sort or the pressure of competition or something. Some cognitive and emotional discovery.

"Respectively," I said, as we got closer, "but is that right, Keiko? Are you okay?"

She looked up a little at her boyfriend and her face dipped in that way of older Japanese women who are on their way to marriage and holding the secrets of their preparedness for this well within.

"O I'm fine, yah," she said. "You know, I think maybe, I am better completely."

"*Oi, yoshi!*" cried Yuko.

"You really had us, Keiko, this time," I said.

"*Hai,*" said Akio. "So now it is all alright. And with your parents too, *kora?*"

"Sure," said Keiko. "Them too."

"Man," said Masami. "you sure were lucky."

"*Hai,*" we all said, in unison.

"Very lucky," chirped her boyfriend, clasping her close now, his left arm looped in her right.

"But who do they think did it?" asked Akio. "Some local boy? A traveller. What?"

She looked at us all coyly and was silent.

"You know," said Kiseki, plumbing forward, smiling, "it is so good to see you all. Because of all this, we haven't yet been able to welcome each other." He bowed to each of us in turn, quite deeply in fact. "Humbly, good to see you all. Keiko and I are pleased of such good friends."

'*Kuso,*" whispered Yuko, under her breath.

"We are. . .' Keiko suddenly chirped, and then stopped and looked up at Kiseki, rolling her lips together. "getting married!"

"*Hai! Hai! Hai!,*" chirped Kiseki, "When Keiko graduates she is going to get a job in Akanyio Bay, and plan to live with me and . . . In two years, when she is seventeen."

"*Ara!*" cried Yuko. "Big news!"

Keiko swung slightly on Kiseki's arm.

"Congratulations," Masami said. "No more thoughts of cooking in *chukka-ryoriya* in Tama for peanuts."

Keiko, smiling.

"Yes, congratulations, Keiko," I said.

"You know, Koji," she said, "you in particular I must thank. So it turns out, yah? You finding me. *Otsukaresama deshita.* All for the best. What about it? It is, humbly, like having a new life."

She stared out past Kiseki in the direction of the International Culinary Institute.

"O . . ." I began, meaning to congratulate her again.

"*Hora,*" she said. "I have to accept it, Koji."

"Keiko . . ." began Nobuko, appearing to reach toward Keiko's arm but suddenly stopping and smiling at her instead.

"Nobuko," said Keiko. "Too sweet, yah. But look at me."

It was true, she still had the appearance of just having been taken from the water, her hair tied roughly behind in and her clothes crumbled.

"How did I . . ?" she said.

"You . . ." I began.

"No," she said, "Koji. Too kind. But I don't remember a thing."

I stared for a moment at her pale lips, not sure if what I was hearing was what she meant. Was she saying that she did not know who did this to her, or that there had been no one else?

"But the police . . . ?" I asked.

"Not going to press charges," barked Kiseki, too brightly.

"What are you talking about?' cried Yuko, in a deeper motherly tone. "*Chotto!* Mad! No charges? What?"

"O," said Keiko. "Please don't be angry, Yuko. I didn't mean to get you all involved. I just . . ."

"You mean . . ." I said, and I imagined Keiko there in the dawn sun, throwing herself into the waters of the Naorai, with the intention of killing herself, and then realised that this was not what she was saying. Rather, she was saying that as she had been "unharmed", and as they had no immediate leads, the police had asked if she wished to proceed and she had answered that she did not.

"Kiseki says I am the luckiest girl here," she said. "I really do think . . ."

"How so," I said. "Keiko . . ?"

Yuko now stepping up closer, little muscles moving in her tiny face as if attempting to transform herself into something more monstrous.

"Keiko must practice," said Kiseki, turning his future bride away toward Harding's punt. "I'm sorry."

'Later, *yah*,' called Masami, as the boat engine coughed into life and Keiko and Kiseki walked off.

"I don't believe that," said Yuko quietly, watching the two of them step down the wooden wharf steps into the punt. 'Married in two years? No, no. I told you that Kiseki is one Kyoto creep, Koji."

"Dasshimen Institute," said Masami, as the punt eased away. "Weird, yah."

A voice suddenly broke in.

Nearby, several cars away but crawling through the car-park, a large American brand of car, a Chrysler I thought, dark silver and enormously curved like a whale or a missile, eased up toward us.

"Nobuko!" the voice called from its rear window. And now a broad arm had emerged and was waving back and forwards in hard, lively jerks.

"Who's that?" I asked.

Nobuko stared as the car rolled up and a face appeared, crowned in a swirl of silver hair, swept back in a cresting wave from the forehead which lunged now toward the open window and cried out again.

"I think," said Nobuko, "it's Uncle Shiro."

7

Ika-osui mono

Of course, some of the greatest cooks of all time have turned out to be the most terrible thieves and the grossest murderers. *Iro wa chairo desu.* A service industry, huh, breeds remorselessness.

Living outside of ordinary experiences, these cooks have given themselves over to uncompromising attitudes. Shinso Miyagawa, for example, who in his *fugu* in Yokote in the mid 1950s cooked nothing but the most poisonous of globefish, sliding lotus root into their beaked humble mouths to hide the curved serrated barbs there and refusing, outright, to slice out the "*kinu*" from the spine, as is the usual practice.

"Impossible, *omagosan*," he would say. "Destroys the flavour."

And so, in his *fugu*, adventurous diners respectfully ate their final meals and, even though they knew as the raw, spiked and gaping fish arrived on its blue plate, beak clamped on the root and body as round and hard as a baseball, that they were about to leave this world, they nevertheless welcomed Shinso Miyagawa to their table so that he could explain the delicate flavour, draw them down into the deep runnels of the fishes' life, tell them of the journey of the spiny school along the *Tsugaru Straits*, through the cold currents that descend from the high latitudes of the Pacific, along the ridges of the Sea of Okhotsk with its high winds that contribute to the heavy snowfalls in northern Honshū and Hokkaidō, and on into the waters around the Kuril Islands, where they were caught, puffing up in the fine fly nets into five times their size, brought gaping and stiff to the markets of Tomakomai, where the chefs of the *ryotei* and *ryoriya* and *nomiya* and *sobaya* of the Obihiro District, a crowd that included Shinso Miyagawa, who sliced the fish open along the belly, removed its internal organs, presenting them in cups of *karashi* and *benisboga* and *takuan*, placed the lotus in its mouth, and served it on a bed of steaming *udon*, so that as the diners listened to this story and took up their *hashi* with which to eat the fish, the grinning face of Miyagawa the chef would be the last face they ever saw.

Fact is, whether in Kyoto or Paris, Wakamatsu or Venice, Sapporo or New Orleans, Yokohama or London, great cooks have proved themselves liable to becoming terrible egotists and impossible megalomaniacs. And not one-off cases only! Again and again, and from all nationalities. This is something a young *rakugo* must accept when he enters cookery: the feeling that you too might turn out to be fussy and bad tempered. Perhaps prove immodest and overly proud. *Kono ressha niwa shukudō-sha ga arimasu ka*. Even worse today, with TV, end up considering yourself a media star! Look, perhaps, at Sumie Mayuzumi. I thought, maybe, of Hiroyuki Imamura. Were these great chefs? Or were these just ordinary cooks with great TV shows? And their books! These were not for step-by-step instruction. A new cook could learn very little from these books. They goaded and challenged and filled the air of cookery with impossible vanity. "You can never," they seemed to say, "sauté a sweetbread quite as delicately as this." "You will never," they cried, "make a soufflé as upstanding." "You truly don't know, do you, how to correctly slice a turbot or how, in fact, to marinate it in tomato and walnut?"

We each hoped none of us would end up like this, crying out in a kitchen at the bad arrangement of sauteuses or the neckerchief we put down and now was lost or the saltiness of the Provencal fish soup or the poorness of the tomato crop.

"I want to be the tenderest of *rakugo*," said Akio, as we waited in the parking lot for Nobuko, who was leaning into what we took to be her uncle's car. "Even baby crabs will want to be cooked by me."

"Some dream," said Yuko.

"Not me," said Masami. "I want to have a big kitchen with several cooking stations and zones for grilling."

"Really," I said, "and who will cook in these?"

"What you think, Koji? Pretty young chefanese."

"*Oya!* Typical. And I suppose," said Yuko, "they will all be your lovers?"

"Masami's *maiko*, yah," said Akio, laughing. "A whole bunch of *nomiya* waitresses."

"Whatever," said Masami, sulking a little, "but at least I have bigger plans than *crab*, Akio."

"What's not big about crab?" said Yuko. "Crabe a la bretonne. Crab farcis a la martiniquaise. . ."

"*Kani-no-sunonomo,*" said Akio.

"Crabes farcis au gratin," said Masami, unable to resist joining in.

"Watercress pancakes filled with saffron crab," continued Yuko.

"*Hai!*" I said. "*Hai!*" But, for the moment, standing watching Nobuko leaning in through the big car's window opposite, I tried to imagine my plans and nothing took shape.

O, it was not that I didn't try. I saw, briefly, a white arched *ryotei* on the banks of Akanyio Bay. It had my name over it and a rooftop made of several cupolas, each of a kind of an opaque green glass that showed the diners within. Perched there in couples, eating who knows what, each of them, these pairs, so engaged with their food that the eating of it seemed in fact to be love itself and their marriage, which I guess is what this food was making, a thing of real harmony. But when I went from this vision to 'my' kitchen it just fell to the floor in a clatter of pans and griddles and flat utensils. I looked around, tried to imagine a larder, a potwash, a vegetable store, a saucier, but at each point my kitchen rose and fell again into rubble, as if it was built on a faultline. It was a relief to hear Yuko's voice, calling to Nobuko as she returned.

"Your uncle?"

The big car was pulling up toward the rock bridge, which had now only barely emerged from the sea making the car, as it reached the rocks, look like it was driving on water.

"His assistant," said Nobuko slowly, reaching us. "He says Shiro-san has invited us all to have dinner with him this evening."

"*Oya!*' we all seemed to say at once. "Unbelievable."

"*Otsukaresama*. Quite an honor," I said, stating the obvious. But Nobuko was abruptly silent, turning to stare across the water toward her Uncle's culinary institute.

"What?" Akio finally broke in, pinching at sweat forming around the stud in her nose. "What is it, *oneesan*? Don't you want to meet your uncle, finally?"

Nobuko, pacing and staring out toward the setting sun, didn't answer.

"Look," said Yuko, "she is probably back in her room, not with that Professor of hers."

"I'm not thinking of my mother, *tori*," said Nobuko.

"Who then?" said Yuko.

Nobuko waited a moment before answering. "My father."

"*Hai!*" I said to everyone. "Nobuko's found out something. Her father, *oya!*, is gay."

"*Chigaimasu*," cried Nobuko. "I don't know that for sure, Koji. I just . . . ."

She looked at me as if I had spoken entirely out of place.

"Forget it," she cried. "I don't know anything."

"But if we don't practice," continued Akio, mentally stirring a pot of tapenade tagliatelle, I think, as if she hadn't heard any of our conversation, 'then how do we hope to pass our cooking exams here?'

"Akio," said Yuko, "can't you see, Nobuko has other things on her mind? Her father, yah."

"You know, Nobuko," replied Akio, still absorbed in seasoning her pot, "your cousin Hiro, respectfully, has enough tattoos to be a big-time criminal. Do you think he is invited tonight?"

Nobuko seemed momentarily about to burst, but the moment subsided and her face, taut beneath her *hachimaki*, grew as round and as flat again as the full Spring moon.

"You don't think he had anything to do with . . . ?" continued Akio.

"How so," I said, "because he frightens you, Akio, you don't want him to meet Shoji-san? Anyway, he was with us."

"*Hai!* Of course." She leant forward as if to sniff the pungent steam of her imaginary pot.

"You know," said Nobuko, staring over at her uncle's institute. "My father has been *kaichoh* and *shachoh* of the Kishimoto Food Company all his life."

"He'll still be *kaichoh*," I said, trying in this to apologise for having spoken so badly out of place.

"A *kaichoh* has no real power," said Yuko. "He's just a figurehead, man. Right Nobuko?"

"That's true," said Akio, suddenly engaged with what we were saying. 'Powerless, yah.'

"Cookingly," said Nobuko. "The direction the company takes will pass to my uncle."

I watched the Kishimoto Food Company team out on the institute's balconies, unfurling banners and stringing these from beams, while a figure that was obviously Shoji stood akimbo on the ground, talking to what was probably the TV crew.

"*Hai!* And guess who is coming?" Nobuko said suddenly, her pigtailed hair no longer swinging back and forth but hanging as still and as heavy looking now as two brown bottles.

"Who?" I said.

"My uncle's assistant swears this is true," she said. "The guest of honor is to be Kyoto Kagawa."

Aenomo

That afternoon, in the mid afternoon sun, golden-brown as a bear and as deep as a cave, Kishimoto Food Company banners began to wave from the balconies, and we worked in the kitchen below them, practising.

Kyoto Kagawa - was this a dream?

I remembered the episode of her TV show when she came on dressed in *yukata* and cooked a *sakana*, which in traditional terms contained local seasonal fish, prawns and crabs but this restriction Kagawa ignored completely and set out with a selection of fishes, both seasonal and preserved, so unknown and so incredible that you could see the audience fearing that when she was finished one of them would be asked to sample it. Elephant trunked fish, humpbacked fish that swam on their heads, clear fish in whom you could witness the mysteries of blood flow and digestion, dog-faced fish, fish stuck with their lips entwined. Or the time she was featured in the "Out and About" pages of *Gendai* for her floor show in the Tsukau Mall, her face made up like a tabby cat and her clothes mostly sheer black rags, her cooking slow-roasted lamb in Greek Kleftico style, talking all the while about the way yoghurt is made in Greece and the interest of the people in body-building. Or the appearances she made on talk shows to reveal the secrets of her complicated love life, which featured TV stars and rock singers and sportsmen and wealthy nightclub owners. Or the impossible popularity of her books which outsold not only the most popular novels and encyclopaedias but likewise the JAF All-Japan Driving Manual.

Some older folks said that Kagawa was brazen and brash and her shows should not be allowed on television.

"*Kono kudamono o okurimono yō ni tsutsunde itadakemasu ka,*" they said. "Worst example of a *shinjinrui.*"

They picketed the TV station where she worked, wearing hachimaki daubed with words like "Decency" and "*Shibafu nite tachiiri-kinshi*' and expressions like "Listen to Us."

"No more Japanese than a Cadillac, yah," they said. "That daughter should have been taught her place. Terrible, bad business."

But the feeling among many people was that Kagawa was just what Japan needed. That she took cookery and made it modern and bright. That she was a young person with energy and vision and should not be held back by old, *rojinrui* ideals. That her sexiness and charm were part of her contribution to new ideals and new ways of thinking.

Flap, flap, flapping in the light breeze: the banners of our sponsors and other Japanese food companies made me think of exactly these things.

Banners promoting cereals and fish, shellfish and confectionary, specialist rices, beer and spirits - including *shochu, jizake* and *awamori* - canned goods from the West, something called *Pop Dogs*, some kind of new meat, and another called *Vytll,* which gave nothing away as to what it was, and crackers and teas, all kinds of teas, and pea and *natto*, and eggs, noodles, biscuits, soft drinks, American coffee, *sembei* crackers, sauces and salts, fruits and meal bread and *kabayaki*.

All those banners along the front of the Institute, chopping up and down, making a kind of clapping noise, as we trainees worked in the kitchens below imagining that we were already following Kagawa's example, imagining what she would say to this.

Akio there trying to form up a potato and shrimp galette on the bench but finding the surface cracked and wondering why. Yuko sweating shallots in butter. Masami slicing bamboo shoots into thin, sinew-like strands. Nobuko filleting along the backbone of a turbot, and sliding the white firm flesh onto the wooden board. Keiko blanching carrots and char-grilling cucumbers. The whole of the kitchen full up with new Institute chef trainees making sauces and marinating meats and fishes, trying out the tools that had been supplied on noodles and fruits and butter and eggs, sifting flour, blending egg and sake and mirin, shredding cabbage, sieving stock, moulding ramekins of lime and salmon and shiitake.

Later that afternoon, with the sunlight fading to a deep fire glow and the kitchens hot with both cooking and conversation, Mr Tieni's instructions began ringing out:

"In order to maintain the standards of Mr Kishimoto Shiro we must at all times be diligent."

He danced past us along the linoleum, in overly long rock star strides, one foot way ahead of the other, swivelling on his boot heels, wearing a gold embroidered chef's coat and neat checked baggies. Though he was rock star, of course, Mick Jager, Eric Clampon perhaps, I thought he looked also like a general; and, also, like a circus trainer; and then also like a madman. Crazy guy.

"Great *rakugo* should be generous with their colleagues, *kodomo-tachi*," he barked, dancing through the kitchen.

He rumbled the stainless steel benches, not from his size, which was quite small, but from the heaviness with which he danced. He seemed to me to be like a storm recently stirring into life and only waiting now for the accumulation of dust and wind and debris and rain to change it into tornado so that it could carry itself further afield.

"Some will win here, some will lose," he said, rumbling past. "But all students of the Kishimoto International Culinary Institute will benefit.'

A troop of uniformed assistants trailed behind him.

"New apprentices should ensure they are clean and prompt," he barked.

He came down through the kitchens and out into the convention room and when the assistants saw us Chefanesee they each bowed slightly lower than usual, which led me to think something as yet unknown was going on.

Uosuki

Out in the convention room Shoji was livid.

"*Aaa!* What is it with Shiro-san, he calls *this* a room? *Wah!* Look at this place! How are we meant to broadcast from here? Too crazy by half, yah. Too . . . it's like the Arabian nights in here. Too . . . dark, *ayu*. It's not right for the Kishimoto Food Company. Not right at all."

His small hands waved around in front of his own small face; his tiny head shaking all its thin grey strands of hair. He reminded me most of an angry mouse; but the fact that he was dying seemed somehow to make him grow. In fact, he seemed at that moment to be larger than the room itself. The famous Wada Shoji who once broadcast such a successful series of advertisements for *MiMi* honey coated *chofu* rice cakes during the Winter Olympics in Sapporo in 1972 that Olympic officials had to ban the brand from events for fear the noise of people eating it would distract the competitors. Who once had teams of young women dressed as tunafish hosting breakfasts in *chikatetsu* stations all over Honshu, to promote a new brand of tuna in tiny resealable pouches, and for weeks people said when they went to take the trains it was just like they were swimming right under the Sea of Okhotsk.

"Big!" he cried in the direction of two carpenters erecting panels making up the face of Yitsuko Sasaki over a table of orchids and lilies and chrysanthemums. "Big as houses, *maa!* You think anyone's going to see what we do here with little flowersies like that? Giant backdrop huh? More flowersies, huh. Go! Do it, do it! That's it."

The room now divided into trade stands and displays; the Golden Valley Tea Company was there, as was Big Boy Seafoods, Tanuki Sweets Corporation, Hokkaidō Ice Supply and the Taifū Beer Company. There were places for each of us at these stands and we could see our Company Representatives each conducting their construction teams who were building. The tea company in giant renditions of tea cups and saucers and a green neon lit hand pouring a steaming brown neon tea to the yellow neon cups below. Big Boy Seafoods: a boy catching a fish which, in glittering green and silver and pink scales of tin foil, tossed and fought and shook. Sweet smelling aromas wafting from the chocolate box that was the Tanuki Sweets Corp stand, traditional *wagashi* and Western sweets too, *chofu* and *yakiimo* and *jonainagashi* sweets, around which no doubt the *kodomo-tachi* of delegates would swarm. The ice castle of the Hokkaidō Ice Supply Company where Keiko would host sushi and sashimi tastings, particularly *chirashi-zushi*, all scattered and bright in deep beds of cold sushi rice.

And ice-sculptures, arranged now on pedestals around the display entrance to represent famous shrines and monuments and historical moments: the Sengaku-ji Temple, Matsumoto Castle, the Seto-Ohashi Bridge near Takamatsu, windsurfing on Lake Biwa. And beside this, strategically placed, the Taifū Beer Company big copper vats from which beer was already being dispensed to display construction workers and the team from the Kishimoto Food Company and those few of Mr Tieni's assistants who had left Mr Tieni's lively entourage and were directing food companies to their designated places in the hall, vans crossing the washy bridge, flat-bed trucks unloading out in the gravelled grounds, the convention hall doors flung open to reversing vehicles and teams of couriers.

"That camera," Shoji cried, and I could see up on the mezzanine a crew of TV technicians wheeling out long lines of cables and cords.

"Greatest food TV," he said, wheeling past me at the kitchen doorway as I stepped out into the room.

"Come, Koji," he called, beckoning me after him. "Look here."

Up on the mezzanine, Mr Teini was lecturing some of the new senior trainees on the procedures for the Parade du Chefs.

"Down this way," he was barking, pointing at the sweeping stone stairs. "Across this way", he slid in guitarist style past the table of official guests, food writers, invited *ryotei* owners, well-known chefs, food company representatives and cultural officials.

"Pause," he said, bowing several times at the judges' table now high at the rear, beneath the arch of the French window.

"And pause once again," he said, bowing deeply at a table where apparently Uncle Shiro himself would be sitting.

"Exit," he said, into the kitchens, where the apprenticeship program would properly begin.

I reached the arched upper windows of the Institute, looking down to the curve of a small bay, with a narrow strip of pearly white sand and the dark still water, and there Shoji stopped and pointed out:

Below on the beach two figures moved in strange leaping steps. For a moment it seemed one was determined to throw itself into the sea, running headlong at the water's edge, raising great sprays of water, and leaping up, up as if to crash down into the sea, only the sea slid back in lapping fashion and the figure landed softly on hard wet sand. And then, raising its arms in complicit flapping, off went the other, the larger of the two, and it would run and run raising even bigger sprays of water, and determinedly so, and then leap, only not so high as the first, and come crashing down with heavy feet, dry nevertheless. And then they ran and embraced, down on the water's edge, standing that way for some time, before they began the whole ritual again.

"I can't complain, huh. *Maa,*" said Shoji. "Wada Shoji has spent a whole lifetime doing his own thing, *chiranade.* Some people have their lives made by others." He watched the pair below beginning their ritual dance again. "Worse for artists, yah. Culinary Arts also. Worse thing in the world to have your life made for you."

Shoga-joya

It was not that I was shocked to be witness to Mrs Kishimoto's dancing with her lover, that prancing, parading beach dance, her nakedness now growing strangely, disconcertingly familiar, only it turned out, Shoji said, that Mr Kishimoto had no idea.

"Too crazy by half, yah," Shoji said, heading off now toward the camera crew setting up noisily on the mezzanine.

This sort of thing was common among Japanese couples of a certain age. Influenced by the popularity of Eastern philosophies in the West during the 1960s period they had reciprocated by taking on Hippy ideals and lived secretly wild lives while the younger of us gave ourselves over to *ringi-sho* and *nemawashi* and ideals of harmony and respect which, though held in the very oldest generation, seemed to have jumped over people of Mr and Mrs Kishimoto's age and landed more heavily on us.

I watched as the sun grew lower on the Naorai's, catching the fishing boats with their lanterns now lit, chugging out from tiny Naorai-go harbour in the direction of the shellfish grounds, their smoke stacks unfurling kites of blue smoke onto the blackening sky, those kites twisting and twirling around each other, slowly sliding away into the night.

Interesting fact: the use of oregano in Japanese cooking was pioneered by chef Susumu Koroda of the Shimogama Hot Spring resort who prepared a meal of *shabu-shabu* for Emperor Hirohito around the time of the Manchurian war of 1931. Poor conditions prevailing, the resort in some need, its gardens being bereft of burdock and ginger, Susumu was forced to rely on a small, soft, mottled-green herb he found growing nearby the rail station, which itself was almost abandoned.

The meal, to Susumu's surprise, was so complimented by the Emperor that Susumu's career was greatly enhanced and some years later in fact found himself chef-du-cuisine of the entire Imperial household. But before this, as that first meal was concluding, and through one of his attendants, the Emperor announced that he was impelled to ask how Susumu Koroda, who was just an ordinary cook in what was merely a small provincial *kyo-kyoriya*, who had not before gained any attention at all for his work or even travelled beyond the Kamo

Province, had been able to make his *shabu-shabu* so distinct, so superior to any other, that it seemed indeed that he alone had the proper recipe for this common dish.

Susumu, of course, was too embarrassed at first to admit that the meal he had prepared for his exalted guest owed its flavour to a ragged plant he had found growing next to the Muroran to Tomakomai rail line. At first he sent the Emperor's attendants back with an unbelievable report that the meal probably owed its extraordinary flavour to a particular sweet kind of beef found in the Chitose district or maybe to the methods his staff had of basting tofu with a wash of kinome leaves. But, when it became clear that the Emperor was growing impatient with this, and in fact questioning the chef's loyalty, he finally broke down and admitted that his *shabu-shabu* owed its uniqueness, its divineness, to a herb he believed Europeans called "oregano." The rest well-known history records as "ingredients: add two leaves of oregano."

Keiko was flapping over her work as I came back into the kitchen.

"Do you think, Koji," she called across the cook top, "we will *all* be great chefs one day, huh?"

I watched her butterfly movements, her blanching of carrots and grilling of cucumbers having turned somehow into a wild mushroom mouse which sat in its terrine as firm and neat as any in history could, but its surface almost like plastic, its color like strangely even tempered mud.

"*Hai!*," I called, nervously, "Surely."

"Surely," Kiseki, echoed, standing watching beside her, "*kokoro*."

"Maybe not all," said Akio quietly, closer by, her potato and shrimp galette now fallen into a rolling waves of white and pink, oozing its failure onto the bench top as she stood over it, a pair of shiny new silver Griefling tongs limp in her right hand.

Out across the expanse of the kitchens the Institute *sensei* were now wandering, casting severe looks on one preparing new cook and another. They looked, respectfully, as if they could be the ghosts of our ancestors recording the undisciplined ways of their sorry dithering relatives, or maybe tornadoes deciding which small coastal town they might set down upon and blow, stick by stick, into the vast ocean of the checkered kitchen floor.

I looked at the rabbit leg that with my own hands I had now boned and dressed, it's thin cartilage handle poking up at the kitchen's ornate ceiling, its saddle rippled with sinew, and the mustard and saffron sauce I had invented to baste it, sitting in white round gratin, a mottle of yellow and orange. Over by the Gastrofast fryer one of the sensei had come across Hiro and, placing his hand right on Hiro's shoulder, was praising his smoky short ribs, for which he was steadily cooking down a chipotle-honey sauce, as one of the finest he had ever seen.

What thing was this, I thought, as Hiro stepped back from the dish and, looking at the sensei as if he had scolded rather than praised him, bowed his head in shame?

8

Mizu-taki

Early that evening, in the east wing of the Institute, the atmosphere was thick with tension. Young cooks, some our age, some just a year or two or three older than us, from Districts as widely separated from each other as Moto-hakone, Wakkanai, Fukui, Saga-ken and Gobō, paced around the corridors or smoked out on the balconies or played hurried, unsettled games of *go*, situating themselves somewhere between knowing each other too well and not knowing each other at all. Sometimes, walking past a group huddled together, or leaning over the balcony rail blowing rings into the night sky, pieces of conversation jumped up like sparks:

". . . . and so use celery seed, maybe, *dansei*. Better flavour, in my view."

"You're kidding me, yah? You really goin' to cook a carpaccio? Brave, man. How you going to sauce your yellowfin— not mozzarella and dill? Argh! Who says . . . ?"

"*Hai!* Agree Kuniko Kuga makes a great bouchèes à la reine. But who in Kyoto does a better *robata-yaki* than Hiroyuki Imamura anyway? I can't agree Shohei-san is in Hiroyuki's league at all."

"I cannot do this," said Akio, watching out from our room to the convention room filling up below with her small thin

face now ashen and eyes flicking back and forth. "*De wa, amata
. . .* I simply cannot do this."

"What's there to do?' I said. "Cook! Cook, huh?"

Akio pinched nervously at the Chefanese golden stud in
her nose.

"*Hai!* Cook," said Masami. "Cook like an American god,
huh, Koji."

"O, sure," I said, "but . . ."

"*Chotto chigaimasu,* Koji," said Nobuko, "Masami-san is
right. We cook now like *Tsukuyomi-no-Mikoto.*"

"Moon goddess?" said Akio, looking frightened.

Nobuko turned to me with a face as fixed and white as a
river stone. "*Cookingly!*" she said, "or else."

Suddenly, outside, below in the grounds of the Culinary Institute, voices started barking. It sounded at first like a rattle of
branches against the big old wooden building, a sudden rush
of sea wind or the gust of a summer gale rising up over the
Naorais. But then, along the rustle, we began to hear words,
and soon we'd each strode out onto the balcony to find out
what they were. All along the balconies, in fact, the trainees,
who were hardly settled anyway, were looking down into the
front garden of Uncle Shiro's Institute.

Almost dark now, the sea had risen to trap the food company vans and flatbeds that had not left earlier, each with its
company emblem on the side, as well as the cars of guests who
had not been brought out via cruiser now tied at the School
wharf, out here on the island, and now all of them unloaded
into the convention room where many of us were due shortly to host their products before retiring to dress in our new
Kishimoto International Culinary Institute coats and baggies and begin the Parade du Chef. Into the kitchens, that is,
where, this evening, we would cook for the first time and, by

the looks of some of us leaning over the balcony rail, perhaps for some it would be the last.

Down below, the sound of the voices grew and, as lights of the Institute stretched out toward the waterfront they caught the figures below on the beach. Not two figures now but three. Two locked arm in arm. Not in embrace. But tightly, shoulder over shoulder, one abruptly swinging the other, then up and over onto the ground, arms and legs now flailing, while nearby the third figure barked out high-pitched instructions and flapped equally, but more expressively, I thought, like a butterfly.

We bound down the stairs, each trainee scrambling after the other, and out onto the front garden.

There in the twilight we could see the three figures illuminated by the waxing moon. One was most obviously Nobuko's mother. She was propped off to one side on one of the large beach rocks, and was trying all she could to unstick the other two with loud, sobbing interjections:

"*Onegai shimasu.* Too awful!" she cried out.

"You think this helps?" she cried.

"*Isha o yonde kudasai!*" she cried.

Finally, Mr Tieni and some of his assistants came running down from the School and dove down onto the beach and, grasping one or other of the wrestlers, pulled them apart.

"There! There! There!" shouted the first of them. It was then we could see that this was Mr Hinds, Nobuko's mother's occidental lover, tall and pasty colored with his grey hair now swooping not back over his large head but down in long bedraggled threads around his now reddened face. "It's him. He attacked Mikko. I think he's the one who . . ."

Mr Tieni's assistants were now restraining Harding who, we could plainly see now, was the other man.

"We were down on the beach,' continued Jasper Hinds, his eyes flashing at Harding, "admiring the new The Moon. I left Mrs Kishimoto alone for five minutes, in order to call my office, and next thing this man appeared and accosted her."

"Lie!" shouted Harding.

"What, you deny it?" Jasper Hinds pulling his hair back over his head, like a veil.

"*Chotto!*" shouted Harding.

"Eiko-san, *onegai shimasu*," he said, in the direction of Mr Tieni. "I have no idea what this man is talking about."

Mr Tieni looked at Nobuko's mother, who had broken down now and was being comforted by Nobuko, clasping her daughter to her and burying her face in her daughter's neck.

"*Koko ga itai desu*," she cried. "Awful! *O, kbun ga warui desu.* What Mr Hinds says is true!"

Temaki-zushi

Could a boy and girl marry I wondered because the boy feels at some point for the girl and gives her comfort, and the girl, struck by the strange turns in her life, her father retiring from his company, the company changing, seeming somehow to turn toward a poor reflection on his time there, her mother, who once was full of great ideas in her own right, taking a lover, the girl's life, which she considered could be devoted to cookery, to cookery that made Japan wake up to the wonders of International cuisine and challenge old notions, celebrated in a spirit of Chefanese adventure and Chefanese excitement, and in this way somehow repair the damage that circumstance and leaving school, maybe, had brought into her life?

Interesting fact: the average educated Japanese person today is said to have had seven serious lovers before they marry. Most being those met during school or in further education. Only twenty-two per cent of young Japanese persons are known to marry someone from outside their town or suburb. Forty per cent of young Japanese today choose not to marry until in their later twenties. The statistics for those who would wish to marry, but have passed by the usual age to do so are varied. Love hotels, prostitution and casual sex do not carry the same overtones as they do in the West.

During the *tomesode* traditional wedding ceremony, the girl still most often wears a *shiromuku*, most often a pure white kimono, while the man wears his formal *moutsuki* kimono bearing the crest of his family. About one-third of marriages in Japan at the present time remain arranged marriages. Usually the match will occur through a relative or family friend. Increasingly computers are used by Japanese grooms to find suitable girls. The average matchmaking agency will charge between ¥350,000 and ¥500,000 for this service. Success rates vary from 15 per cent to 35 per cent. Introductions are made via emails and recorded voice, which saves the client from embarrassment and increases the opportunity for choosing the most suitable partner. Today, the *hiroen* ceremony is most often held in a hotel. Gifts of money, in *depato* envelopes, vary in size. The average *depato* contains a gift of between ¥30,000 and ¥50,000. Rental of the *shiromuku* will cost the bride and groom's families in the vicinity of ¥200,000. The over all cost of the wedding ceremony will be in the vicinity of ¥600,000. Far less food is consumed than at Western weddings.

However, in all this, despite these differences and preferences, the wedding cake, with its high topped syllabub-like mountains, whirling around one layer at a time, higher and higher, higher than Fuji-san, its golden plastic arches on top, its couple in their plastic clothes walking through, neatly embracing each other in pink smiling happiness, is a similar feature.

The assistants had Harding between them, at least nominally appearing to hold him there. But subtlety was respectively needed. I have no doubt that the thoughts I was having of somehow saving Nobuko from the embarrassment of what was happening, of lifting her out of that moment and bringing her back to us Chefanese, was shared also by Akio and Masami and Yuko. Though I suspected, for the first time, that perhaps my feelings were stronger.

Keiko, meanwhile, had turned her face away and was being led away by Kiseki who was telling her the best she could do was to try and compose herself for the night ahead and whatever happened else-wise could be put aside until later.

"My God!" said Yuko later, "and that man standing there denying it!"

"*Hai!* I'd have punched his lights," said Masami, uncharacteristically.

Still insisting he had done nothing, Harding was escorted by Mr Tieni and his assistants to the Institute's office on the upper floor of the Institute. Away, of course, from the activities which were unfolding in the convention room. For further discussion.

Jasper Hinds comforting Mrs Kishimoto, and the other trainees now hurrying back to their rooms to prepare, I stood with Nobuko on the water's edge and waited for her to speak.

"Do you think . . ?" she said finally, not really needing to expand any further on the question, her eyes expanding enough in their reflections of the water.

"I'm not sure," I admitted. "The boatman? Removing women's clothes? . . . What does your mother say?"

"She doesn't want to speak about it. She says I should concentrate on my studies."

"*Hai!*" I said, "that's some thing. How . . . ?"

Nobuko drifted along the sand slightly, looking from the dark water up to the lit rooms of the Institute where the other trainees could be seen running back and forth past the lighted windows in various stages of chef dress.

"He didn't touch her," she said, word-choosing. "Only made suggestions."

"*Oya!*" I said. "But enough is enough. So you don't think . . ."

"About Keiko?" she said, and looked straight at me with eyes still and reflective. "No. A local boy, the police suspect."

"*Hai!*" I said, and tried to find the lights of the bay some twenty miles back along the Naorais but could only make out the bobbing lights of the evening fishing boats, trawling up the waters for trigger fish and turbot and hake.

"Bad omen, Koji?" she said. "First Keiko and now my mother? I mean," she said, "Out here, Koji, it is very different from Akanyio Bay."

"Yes," I said.

Night on the Naorais seemed to be rolling in across the water so incredibly fast, pushing the orange dusk not exactly out of the District; but, rather, toward its extremities, the lights of the tiny towns and pine forests, harbours and islands, and the city much much further away, to the west, sparkling but only dimly, forcing it onto the horizon, ringing us in orange now, as if the night was larger and more encompassing than any possible day, pluming itself into the space that gentle day had more simply occupied, and pushing it further and further away.

Behind us food companies, declaring the quality of their hosts, some of whom, like us, were formally entering the Institute tonight, had attracted the guests onto the extremities of the convention hall, its bright lights now sparkling out its huge latticed windows and onto the neat grass of the island. Our own stands were waiting, Nobuko's with its *muguicha*, its *matcha*, its *hojicha*, *genmaicha*, *sencha* and *gyokuro* teas, in jute sacks upon sacks so that the guests here, some who were food purchasers from large grocery stores, some chefs themselves, some wholesalers and some food producers and manufacturers, could smell the quality of the teas of the Golden Valley Tea Company. Likewise, Akio and I were due shortly at the stand of the Big Boy Seafood Company and there, being broadcast now from the camera crew of Wada Shoji, was the man I recognised as the company's regional, Hokkaidō manager, a large, slow-slung, joking man called Sugioka, who rarely found his way to any Big Boy promotions, but when he did seemed to be the Big Boy, himself, loud and with hands clasping enormously those closest to him, a former *yokozuna* sumō wrestler, Akio claimed, whom she'd seen fighting, she was sure, for the Kokugikan stable in Sapporo, and who now devoted himself to fish:

"Find better *ika* than ours. *Iie!*" he said toward Shoji's camera. "No chance. The salmon fishes love us."

He thumped out from the stand, rocking back and forth, with what looked like a sheet of *sayori no shio-yaki* garfish in his hands for passers-by to sample.

"Sea bream swim up to our Big Boy ships. *Ōke!*"

Now shouting at the guests wandering in, and for the camera:

"We are close friends with sea urchins so our *uni* is unassailable!"

This scene, and Masami's company, Tanuki Sweets Corporation, now passing out candied chestnuts, *uji* ice and strawberry jelly, and Keiko's and Yuko's companies also opening for business. The hall seemed suddenly very full, because of this, the guests now milling more thickly around each stand and, observing the steady stream of arriving *sensai* in their fine red and blue *yukata,* chatting and pointing and laughing. Because of this, or because, finally, the time had finally now come, the thuds of a *o-daiko* drum began.

First one strike. Then two. Then three in succession. Then a single two-three timed beat. Leading, now, to a familiar rhythm . . .

That sound, the low, rhythmic meeting of wood with wood, each stroke hanging precisely in the air, each echoing in the convention hall and out into the dark water of Naorais, announced that it was time for the Parade du Chefs.

Sayori no-suzuke

And so, we came in along the mezzanine, the Kishimoto International Culinary Institute echoing with drum *o-daiko* noise.

Mr Tieni's assistants instructed us to make two full passes of the room, and then in through the red *minka*-rooved tent, its decorations of birds and rice and stars to offer good health and good luck, hiding the kitchen doors. The first pass to present ourselves to the exhibitors, the guests and the Institute staff. The second to be formally welcomed by the Institute Director.

I thought Akio looked at that moment like the most perfect Kyoto *geiko*, her face white as lilies, her steps short, a little fast, sure, but steady. Shoji's broadcast confirms this. Masami, too, seems taller on screen than he really was and older all of a sudden, proud, perhaps even too proud, his parents visible by the doorway, clinging arm in arm, driven in that afternoon from the Hinomoto District, on the outskirts of Akanyio bay, where families like Masami's, with their new industrial wealth, his father in the transportation business, had begun settling in the late 1970s. Yuko moves jauntily, smiling even, her father grinning back, while Nobuko seems surprisingly awkward and nervous, with her own mother standing among Mr Tieni's assistants, but no sign of her father, and Jasper Hinds and Mr Tieni equally invisible. My own parents, *otoosan* and *okaasan* Kendall, who never thought their *gaijin* son would devote himself to Japanese kitchens and cookery, who had often speculated that my interest lay in electrical things or the law, who dreamt maybe of me working for NTT or the Kuroda Corp., stand there by the Big Boy Seafood stand, Sugioka with them, my father engaging in some sort of conversation with the former sumō, his own round bald head bobbing along in quiet agreement with Suguioka's much heftier one, talking about who knows what, but watching me all the time to the point that I wondered, despite his literary interests, had my father found in this cookery now something to admire? My mother, surprisingly broad-shouldered for a woman, had her hands clasped in front her in that manner she had of capturing whatever was bothering her into her square hands and wringing it out.

And there, as we stepped down onto the convention hall floor, the drumming of the *o-daiko* stopped and the single sound now was our walking in neat file passed parents and now the School *sensai*, passed School assistants and now food company stands, the younger hosts who were not this year entering the Culinary Institute, or who had not succeeded in their applications, or who, in fact, did not consider cookery their lives but only a passing thing that they were doing before entering Meiji University or Kyoto or Sapporo or joining a company. At each we stopped, bowed low, greeted them with *'Itsumo osewani natte orimasu, I'm sorry for the inconvenience'* and then continued. Until we were past all this and turned again, this time with the kitchen doors firmly in front of us.

There was one final turn each new student, apprentice or trainee, had to make, a final and most important pause, before we entered the Institute's kitchens and passed into the training ahead. The turn, that is, to Kishimoto Shiro, Nobuko's uncle, who apparently would be waiting at the doors to the Institute kitchens to welcome us personally. All around, the banners of the Kishimoto International Culinary Institute, banners of prawns and lobsters, daikon, pepper, carrot, cabbage, red beans, seaweed, sweet potatoes, hung long down the walls. The *o-daiko* drum again sounding out. And again. And then we were inside the *minka* and we could see the shape of him at the other end of the tent.

It seemed to me, then, that we had entered some new world, a Japanese world and a chef world equally. That all this talk of being Chefanese would or would not become a real thing. The Shimura Junior High School now gone forever. And Uncle Shiro's International Culinary Institute now in front of us. A world from which we could only emerge altered somehow. Each lantern along the tent shining in dim red, like an artery of light leading out from some enormous culinary heart. And the drums now drumming faster outside as the audience, no doubt, observed the dark shape of us moving upward along the tent corridors. Hiro behind me. And, behind him, Akio and Yuko, then Keiko, some others, and then Masami and Nobuko. As we neared the kitchen doors I thought for a moment that should Nobuko and I get closer perhaps, become lovers, marry, have children, that the shape of our group would be changed, and maybe would never again be the same. But time would tell this. For now, hardly humble at all in our Kishimoto International Culinary Institute coats and checked baggies, we stepped forward toward Kishimoto Shiro, who sat silent near the doors. And why . . . ?

Kishimoto Shiro, his face disfigured into lines of raised pink flesh, his blind eyes behind black glasses, his ears warped and unhearing, he could neither hear us nor speak to us, but reached out his right hand and, using the touch of gauze-covered fingers alone, silently welcomed us to his esteemed cookery school.

Diary

14 years old, I wrote in my diary:

"Cookery today is everything to me. I have today finally decided this. Cookery! Cookery! Cookery!

"Cookery is complication. It is the tangle of importances we attach not to one thing but to many things, and must unravel but not break to come to understand. Cookery is not magic or simply great human labor but the adventure of consideration where no thing is only its material worth, say the flavor of a spice of the texture of a fish, but the suggestion it brings to a dish, the inclinations it induces in the eater. In this way it is more than an illusion and is not improved either only by effort. I think an example of this is that on its own a flavor or a texture is only one thing, with other ingredients these become almost infinite things, a universe of things. Such is the true nature of cookery. Without cooking, nothing. With cooking, only then a thing that must be eaten away. It is perfect!

"Cookery is conversation without words and an activity that brings about your otherwise yet unknown feelings. Cookery is the nightly drift of cedarwood smoke from a salmon fishery on the nearby wharf. So familiar it is that it is like the scent of your mother, comfortingly present even when absent, a memory and a call out from your nearby Bay house. But cookery is surprise too, the unexpected and unfathomable, whose existence maybe you questioned until you tasted how shrimp is in browned butter and red-grapefruit, or the way oil and water can mix when mustard is added, or the speed with which almonds are ground in a *surikogi*, or what lime scent can accomplish when added to a green tea mousse. Then it is gone.

"Cookery reminds us, *yah,* that all around there is joy! Desire! Passion! Happiness! Determination! Love! Laughter! These things.

"So now I begin my apprenticeship.

"Today I become a Japanese cook."

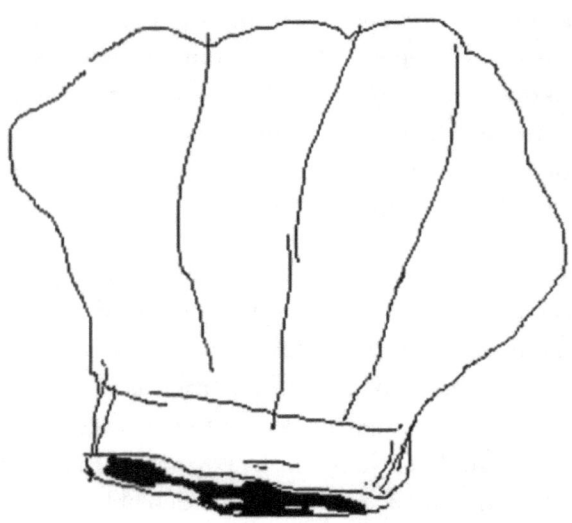

Acknowledgments

To the cooks of *Kore Wa Honmonode Wanaidesu,* who brought such wonders to the table, and regularly took me back into the kitchens too, thank you! *Doumo arigatou gozaimasu!* Without you none of this book would have been possible. I particularly enjoyed discussing the *Kimchi Nabe* and sincerely applaud you again for adding an onion. *Doumo* also to the cooks of *Tsukurimono,* Two Dog Fish, The Peacock Parade, *Kyōryū Bāgā,* Biggy Luna, The Glazed Joint, *Jūten Ga, Hiiku* and Braised Braised for your friendship, your kindness, and your cookery!

Osoreirimasu likewise to Professor Tom Hope, who introduced me to his many thoughts on the differences in studying and teaching literature in Japan when still new and unaware of much of the language and culture. My bag and wallet are still missing, Tom, but the experience of your insights lives on and your contribution to shaping that experience cannot go unmentioned here. To Lydia Montrose of the Department of English Language and Literatures at Naoshima University also. I am sure the magnificent mysteries of the Inland Sea will soon be evident to all, Lydia.

Thanks to the librarians of the National Library of Kuid-aore - Himoti, Michiko, Mizuki, Takuma. *Doumo ariga-tou gozaimasu!* I could have stayed forever in those archives, as you know; not least because of your wonderful support and companionship.

To Dave Blakesley, who never ever fails to get things cooking! Who keeps things boiling, serves up the most un-expected of delicacies, hosts dinners of champions and feasts unimaginable, has great taste, and never fails to make every-one feel at home around the table. Simply, a great publisher! Thanks Dave.

Finally, to Louise, and to our sons Myles and Tyler— truly great travelers to places both real and unreal. Loving you always.

About the Author

Graeme Harper (writing as Brooke Biaz) is a fiction writer and critic. He is Editor-in-Chief of the international journal, *New Writing*. His awards include the National Book Council Award for New Fiction (Australia), among many others. A member of the Welsh Academi and a former Commonwealth Universities scholar in creative writing, he is a Fellow of such organizations as the Royal Society for the Arts, the Royal Society of Medicine and the Royal Anthropological Institute. He has held professorships and honorary professorships in a number of universities in the USA, Britain, and Australia, and was the inaugural chair of the Higher Education Committee at Britain's "National Association of Writers in Education" (NAWE). He is founder/director of the annual "Great Writing International Creative Writing Conference", held each year at Imperial College, London. He is Dean of the Honors College at Oakland University, Michigan, USA. Among his other works are *Cinema and Landscape*, with J.R.Rayner, *The Invention of Dying*, and *Small Maps of the World*.